House of Harrow

CASSANDRA CELIA

HOUSE of HARROW

Cassandra Celia

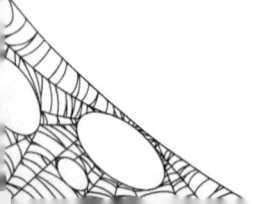

Also by Cassandra Celia

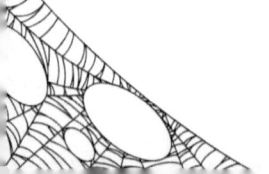

Contents

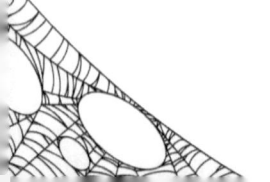

Caution!

By reading past this point, you are recognizing that HOUSE OF HARROW is an adult book that features mature and at times triggering themes and material. For a complete list of relevant content warnings, please visit my landing page located at the end of this book.

We are all in control of our own content consumption.

Thank you, and I hope you enjoy!

For those who loved something so much that you destroyed it.

Part One

"And there she lullèd me asleep,
    And there I dreamed—Ah! woe betide!—
    The latest dream I ever dreamt
    On the cold hill side."

-La Belle Dame sans Merci: A Ballad, John Keats

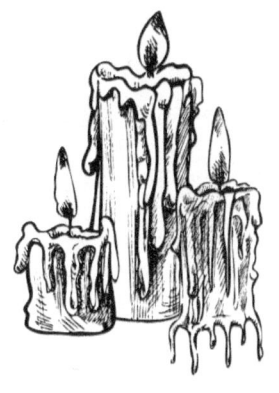

Chapter 1
The Crow

YOU COULDN'T HEAR THE SCREAMS FROM THE CHILDREN LIVING inside the house on the hill. Though the walls were not thick, their cries were snatched from thin air and stripped, until nothing was left, no lingering trace remained. Sometimes, if the wind hit just right, you could lean your head in and catch the remnants of a shriek, but otherwise, their voices were stolen by the air currents and swiftly subdued.

The house stood tall and narrow, its joints and corners a collection of angles that couldn't have aided its stability. One wrong brush of a hip and the entire place might have collapsed. Still, it endured, a true testament to its resilience. Even after years of rot and decay, the house on the hill prevailed; the splintered wood that kept it together withstood the test of time. It lingered out of spite, remaining, at its core, a punishment to all those who ignored it.

Regardless, the reasons for its solitude didn't matter. It was home to lost children; the abandoned, the unwanted, the dispensable. The house belonged to the children who lived there—it survived so long as their beating hearts fed it.

And the hearts were never in short supply.

Perched atop the highest windowsill of the belvedere, a crow cloaked in onyx stretched his wings, staring from the roof, cresting out into the forest. Here, he was at home, content in the house's desolate company, despite the roughness of the fish scale shingles that lay atop the dormer, and the wind that stole the children's screams. Mayhem was almost a part of the house himself, cemented to the windowsill for days on end. He was unafraid of the house on the hill.

Mayhem opened his beak and released a *caaaw* that mimicked the cries coming from inside, his snapping beak and angry ruffled tail feathers willing his admonishment to travel with the wind to those that cowered below the hill, recoiling in their fear.

They deserved no less for abandoning the children trapped within—to ache from the sound.

"Come, bird, quiet your squawking," a tight, scorched voice said from just inside the window. Her voice sounded as though it had lived for a hundred years or more; an aged voice, used sparingly out of fear of each flammable word charring her throat.

It caused the crow to shake out his feathers in frustration as he turned to face the crone. Mayhem cocked his head, his beady eyes focusing on the face he'd come to know so well. He was a fraction of her size and high in the window out of reach, but she could grab him should she wish. The woman's eyebrows drew tight, accenting the wrinkles on her forehead more prominently, and her mouth thinned into a white line.

She might have been pretty at some point in her life, but time had not been kind. Her mouth drooped at the corners, pulling into her familiar scowl. Her nose, once long and pointed, sagged, and several large divots blemished her skin.

The crone's face always appeared to be melting. Skin dripped from her chin, elongating those once beautiful features into something grotesque as it seeped to the floor, hardening like freshly poured candle wax. She constantly changed throughout the years, partly from the decay of time, but most prominently from her unwavering state of deliquescence.

In all her forms, Mayhem would know the witch, Harrow.

From his perch, he noted the remnants of her waxy debris across the room; years of sticky sap coating the floor, layered with a thinly veiled film of dried beetle carcasses and half-living flies that caught in her tacky web. There was almost no floor left to be seen, hidden underneath Harrow's cocoon of dirt, grime, and wax.

Her most frightening features, the crow believed, were her lack of eyes. No glowing bulbs sat on either side of her nose but hollowed raw sockets instead. Caked inside, an aged spiderweb fluttered strands of silky threads, strings of it swaying while she stumbled around, as if she never had any eyes at all. Pain and rage swam within their depths, circling sharks ready to feast on whatever chump laid out before them.

Even without her eyes, Harrow knew all who walked her halls. She knew which children scurried from room to room, and the critters that hid behind the walls. Harrow was the keeper of the house on the hill and had been for as long as the oldest tree in the forest surrounding it.

The house never answered to anyone but her; it would always be hers, above all else.

"You must eventually leave the safety of your window,"

she snarled, her voice full of croaking threats, "and you will find the back of my golden cage. It's been primed for you for far too long, dear bird." Her hand pointed towards the corner of the room, and Mayhem's head tracked the ends of her long, slender fingers. The flames at each tip flickered aggressively, illuminating the gilded bird cage.

Mayhem clicked his beak. He was not a pet and never would be, not after the horrors he had seen happen in that very cage. Instead, he continued to stare, blinking as little as he could allow, for fear that she would break their truce. Mayhem was free to wander, free to watch over what occurred in her lair, until he came to her willingly.

She would never grab him; not like she did the children. He often wondered why she afforded him that choice, but it served him well to be wary.

His claws tapped impatiently on the wood, ready to jump if the need to flee surfaced.

Harrow *tsked*, bringing her hand close to her chest. The orange glow of fire that danced around each candlestick finger burned holes through her dirtied tunic, although that didn't appear to bother her. Mayhem shook his small body again, spreading his wings to combat his nerves. Her empty sockets bored into his chest, and she laughed, croakily, the horrific sound filling the room. The noise rang sharp and pointed, slicing through the air, digging its painful blade into Mayhem's heart.

"For a bird that humanity fears as a bad omen, you are not the scary little thing they think you are."

Though his breathing was even, Mayhem's heartbeat raced. He might not embody the dreadful darkness of his kind, but she was the epitome of every dark rumor whispered about her.

Harrow turned from the crow and shifted slowly away

from him. She blew out the fire lit across her fingertips and wiped the melted wax on her clothes. Without another word, the keeper of the house on the hill retreated deeper into her hell home, leaving dried wax footprints, and Mayhem, in her wake.

Chapter 2
The Rat

THE HAG'S MAZE SPRAWLED, FULL OF NOOKS AND CRANNIES.

As Flea scurried across a hallway, splinters dug into the soft pads of his feet, scarred from his years of flight. The boards were rough, especially around through-holes in the baseboards, as he bolted through one into the comfortably close squeeze of the walls, reemerging into another large open human space.

No one was left to care for the maze the way it required. The groundskeepers had died long ago when the trees that outlined its perimeters were nothing but saplings. And that *hag*, the child snatcher, the children eater, the crone made of wax, had done nothing to preserve the integrity of it.

He sat on a decaying beam, his beady eyes recording the slow disappearance of the once beautiful maze. Years of neglect had taken their toll, revealing cracks and crumbles in the foundation, chipped paint and rotting wood. Peeling wallpaper sagged from the walls, and the jagged shadows cast by broken windows were left unattended, as if the maze itself mourned its own demise. Flea tracked every crevice and noted every new disturbance. The maze had gone from a beautiful articulation of human ability to a haunting reminder of human failure, a shadow of its former self.

As he scurried along, Flea passed by abandoned furniture and the broken rubble of what used to be cherished possessions, now strewn about like discarded toys. A faint taste of must lingered in the air, tangible on his whiskers.

He had forgotten how long he lived here; the only indication of passing time was how much duller the maze became. Time did not exist in this place. It was its own portal in the universe, a pocket that opened just for terror, a place for the hag to feed. Flea should never have come here.

Even though the rat had no one alive to return to, he desperately tried to find ways to escape. The temptation of feeling the wind and the sun on his fur rallied him onward, though it proved too elusive as time crawled on. The space he had run through for years now moved too often. Doors he once remembered were long gone, disappearing silently as more nightmares arrived.

Harrow liked to toy with her food, sending monsters and demons to hunt them if she was feeling playful, and moving rooms as she saw fit. To confuse all who travelled them.

The rat felt trapped.

He was used to the Hag's tricks, and as he maneuvered through the thin walls—his skinny body slipping between drywall and wood paneling—he didn't panic. Flea wasn't trying to find the route to freedom today; it felt so out of reach that he had only one thing on his mind.

The children.

He wasn't particularly fond of children, but seeing as they were his only company in the labyrinth, he had very few choices. He couldn't talk to them, not in their language, but their bodies were enough to soothe him. They suffered in this place together, and the rat reasoned that the longer he remained with them, the sooner he would find a way out. It had been years since he truly believed that, but his hope kept him searching for them within the maze.

Hope was the Hag's favorite power to wield.

Though the number and faces ebbed and flowed, the children she stole were plenty. Dropped into this place like pawns in a game of chess, fear and dread always lingered on their tongues, its metallic flavor tasting of defeat and resignation. It was a game of halls and terrors that devoured them whole, leaving nothing but their splintered bones. Children came, but none would survive long enough to really make an impression.

Flea cocked his head, straining to hear any trace of them. The children were quiet tonight, though not for long, he assumed. The quieter in the maze it was, the keener the Hag would be to find them.

In the dark she came for you, she took you, and you never returned.

Flea's whiskers twitched, a ritual flick to rid himself of the layers of wax that settled over his snout. Its invisible strands dripped from wooden beams overhead, pooling like viscous tears. Each lump and drip told a story of anguish, a twisted narrative etched in layers of hardened sorrow. Some were marred with the faintest hints of color, like dried blood staining a pale canvas, while others appeared eerily pristine, as if they were waiting for the next soul to succumb to their pull.

His rounded ears flexed, his body immediately still as they caught whispers of children drifting from inside a nearby room. Flea felt relief, though he knew it would be short-lived. The Hag could sense any trace of jouissance in her labyrinth and smothered it upon discovery. Regardless, the rat allowed a deep breath to fill his narrow body. It infused his lungs and pressed against his ribs, and was the closest he could feel to genuine comfort again, if only for a moment.

The children's whispers grew louder as he approached, frantic in his attempts to find a connecting hole through the drywall leading to them. He was not usually the type to feel so claustrophobic, but so much time spent in the maze of the walls settled over his heart like a constant grip of unending pressure, making him erratic and paranoid. The house liked to play tricks; it enjoyed his torment.

Just past a bend in the floorboards, Flea spied his opening. It was smaller than he remembered but was still large enough for him to push through. A tight squeeze, even for something as thin and fragile as he was.

His shoulders slumped, the tight knot of fear in his belly unraveling. *Relief.*

As the rat approached the hole in the wall, he pressed his chest to the floor and flattened himself as much as he was able. He used all four paws to shimmy his way through the opening to the other side. It took a little effort, and by the time he escaped the walls, it left him heaving.

Flea raised his head and his nose tasted nothing but staleness. The children hadn't found anything to eat today, and that meant he wouldn't be eating again, either. His stomach rumbled in protest, but he ignored it.

Five children sat cross-legged, making a small circle in the middle of the room. Flea's small nails skittered along the wood as he ventured into the open, feeling the coolness of the floor beneath his paws, each step lighter than the last, staying close to the walls as he searched the perimeter.

Nothing threatening presented within his line of sight, but you could never be too sure.

He couldn't get too attached to them, as much as their numbers fluctuated, but he was particularly drawn to this bunch.

One of the children, a girl no older than eight, smiled as she noticed him. Flea heard her whisper something to the others, and each turned their heads to greet him. She had a mess of curly brown hair that framed her face like a lion's mane. Her large, inquisitive blue eyes darted around the circle, following every slight movement. She sat with her legs pulled close to her chest, her sneakers glowing faintly under the dim light, twirling a bracelet on her wrist nervously, her face a mix of curiosity and caution.

"Flea!" A boy to the right of the girl grinned as the rat approached, holding out his hand for him to climb up. He was lanky, with knees that stuck out awkwardly from his too-short jeans. His blonde hair, messy, was stuck to his forehead, which was perpetually furrowed, as though deep in thought—or deep in worry. A smudge of dirt stained his cheek, and he fidgeted with the hem of his faded hoodie, its sleeves fraying from being pulled too often. The Lanky Boy seemed to look past the others, even as his eyes watched Flea, scanning for something unseen.

Flea touched his cold nose to the boy's warm palm. When he looked up, he noticed several small smiles from the others within their circle.

He was a welcome guest here; that was good. The rat appreciated their company in return.

"We hadn't seen you today, you worried us." Lanky Boy lifted his hand to eye level and Flea stared at him. Flea was afraid that even the tiniest of squeaks would ruin the moment, where they welcomed old friendships instead of being just survivors. Even if he didn't speak to them, he hoped they could feel his warmth.

Lanky Boy let Flea climb up his arms, and the rat settled in the crook of his shoulder, wrapping his tail around the flesh of the boy's neck.

"You haven't missed anything," he continued, letting his voice trail off, his sentence unfinished. Flea understood. They were all afraid to speak too loudly, worried they would reveal their hiding place, hoping that the Hag would not find them.

Lanky Boy was fairly new, finding his way to the maze just two weeks ago. It was the longest the Hag had gone without taking a new child, and the anticipation of who they would find next—and subsequently who they would lose—loomed over all the living things inside the maze.

They were all frightened, and the rat could sense by the boy's tightened muscles and shallow breathing that he wasn't adjusting well. He loved Flea, though. And while the rat promised himself that the attachment was foolhardy, it was hard not to lean into that affection.

The messy haired girl—Blue, he named her—smiled at Flea in the surrounding silence. He didn't want to learn their names. It was too dangerous to have more than a miniscule amount of fondness, and so the rat remembered them for their most prominent attributes instead.

It was easier to mourn someone you didn't care for.

The smallest of the group, Smalls, had tanned skin that glowed in the faint light and wide, alert eyes that looked almost too big for her round face. Her braided pigtails were tied with bright red ribbons, a sharp contrast to her quiet demeanor. She sat perfectly still, her hands folded neatly in her lap, though her fingers trembled ever so slightly.

Greasy sprawled out lazily, his body language the exact

opposite of the others' tense postures. His shaggy black hair that was as slick as oil, hung over his eyes, a dimple on one cheek deepened every time he smirked. He wore an oversized t-shirt that looked more like a hand-me-down from an older sibling, with a faded logo stretched across it.

The only other boy that Flea knew almost nothing about, sat with his hands clenched tightly around the arm of his small, stuffed bear, as if it was his only lifeline. Bear's strawberry-blonde hair was tied into one knot at the base of his neck. His freckled face looked pale, his green eyes darting nervously toward the walls. Though his bright shirt seemed out of place in the dreary room, its cheery pattern clashed against his anxious energy.

Blue looked at Flea with a softened expression, the crystal color of her iris' glistening as he stared back from Lanky Boy's shoulder. She had been here the longest out of this group of children, and her and Flea's familiarity weighted their understanding of one another in unspoken words.

Lanky Boy would not last long if he couldn't get himself under control, either killing himself in the process, or all of them.

It was easy to see how close he was to falling apart already. His shoulders shook, subtly, and though his voice sounded cavalier, the tremble in it could not mask how close he was to ruin. Flea believed that everyone who sat within their circle sensed it, no matter how fervently he tried to hide it.

Tears welled at the corners of her eyes, and Blue blinked several times. Flea looked away, lifting his snout into the air, and pretended to find something more interesting than her fear-stricken face. His claws tightened around corded muscle, eyes scanning the room, not the children. He couldn't bear the morbidity.

Flea jumped from the boy's shoulder and curled up in the center of their circle, where they reached out to comfort him. Fingers slid along his back, nails scraping against dried wax from his pelt and slicking the fur he'd already groomed back repeatedly. For a moment, everything was quiet, and Flea allowed himself to close two of his three eyelids. Behind them were vivid images of the fields, flowers, and burrows of his youth.

He couldn't fall asleep, that too was too dangerous, but, at least, he could imagine that this was a place full of light and solace. Flea could pretend that he wouldn't die here, in the maze that trapped him.

Chapter 3
The Crow

THE STING OF A COLD BREEZE RUFFLED THE CROW'S TAIL FEATHERS, yet Mayhem welcomed the distraction, flowing through his black down to embrace his bones. He perched on the highest windowsill, watching Harrow through slitted eyes. With each blink, his gaze would fog, stripping her down to nothing but a silhouette. It allowed him a moment of reprieve; he was robbed of rest beyond the hill. Here at the house, he could watch her, if nothing else.

It wasn't as if he could do anything; he couldn't save the children she brought back here or keep them away from her clutches. Maybe watching, and bearing witness to the atrocities was enough, something to balance his feelings of inadequacy at his inability to protect the children; that this would not be forgotten.

Sometimes the crow worried he only stayed so close to the house on the hill because he and Harrow were friends— that he could not bear the thought of friendship so much, that he stayed exclusively in the company of someone like her. Or worse, that there wasn't a soul in the world who could tolerate the thought of friendship with him.

Mayhem worried that, through his inaction, he was just as bad as the woman made of wax, the one who resided in the hell house.

Harrow.

She paced back and forth in her room, trails of wax abandoned to harden on the surrounding carpet. At one point in time, it had been a beautiful emerald green, deeply pigmented, rich with expensive threads woven into its seams. The whole house had been that way, lavish and overindulgent, with crystals dripping from chandeliers, and decadent tapestries that emboldened the walls. Beautifully overdone, in ways that seemed garish to an untrained eye.

But to someone like Harrow, it facilitated her facade. Though she herself was not decadent, her house's perception had a reputation; one that kept her hidden for decades. The villagers would not bother her, not while her home looked like something from another time. Something out of their reach.

Now, years later, the walls lay barren. The crystals had long since fallen and shattered, shards ornamenting the floor, waiting to be crushed beneath soft feet and tender nerves. Everything about the house nestled on top of the hill aged terribly. Dirt and grime covered every surface, and wax caked so deep into the carpet that it lost its coloring, weathered from browned footprints and blackened time.

In its negligent state, no one approached the house, which remained a monument. Her home, even in its rot, remained inaccessible—a masterful deception.

Harrow's pacing always set Mayhem into an unyielding trance. He watched her prowl back and forth. The crone paused every so often to listen for idle, hiding children. It was her favorite game to play.

This was how she passed time in the house, when not

following the lure of pursuing the children. Nothing but the gentle sweep of her bare feet across the carpet disturbed the silence, back and forth, her feet kicking up wedges of wax with sharpened toenails. If she clipped the pads of her feet with fallen crystals, she gave no reaction, no flicker of pain crossed her slipping, dripping face. Instead, her mouth twisted into a smile so grotesque it looked as if it were carved by a madman. Wisps of brittle hair framed her pallid visage, matted and tangled remnants of a long-forgotten nightmare. Her skin gleamed with a sickly sheen, emphasizing the cavernous hollows of her empty eye sockets, which seemed to pull in the surrounding darkness, with cracks spider-webbed across her forehead.

Mayhem wasn't certain that Harrow was capable of feeling pain.

"If you keep looking at me that way, bird, I'll pluck your eyes out."

The croak of her voice pulled him from his illusion. Mayhem clicked his beak and shook out the staleness in his feet.

He quite liked his eyes, just as they were.

Jumping from the sill right into the house, he hopped until he found himself on top of her gilded cage while Harrow paced several yards away. He'd be able to fight free of her grasp if she tried to come for him; at least, that was his hope.

She wouldn't, he knew. As unlikely as it sounded, Mayhem trusted her word. Harrow would not trap him unwillingly, as she did her prey. Nevertheless, he made sure his claws wrapped loosely around the bars, staying as far away from the cage's open door as possible.

So long as he could see her clearly, he would be safe.

Harrow paid his position on top of her cage no mind as

she continued pacing. A crater would form in the ground if she walked that same path one more time.

"All's been quiet in the house, hasn't it, Mayhem?"

The crow's eyes blinked slowly, his mouth opening to squawk at her indifferently.

"Too quiet, really."

Harrow completed another round of pacing, bringing her wax fingers to her lips to dampen the wicks that resided on each fingertip. Mayhem watched as the flames flickered before disappearing, fresh steam wafting into the air around them, cloaking her hands in a fog of smoke. She turned to face him, a stroke of horror stretching across her weathered face. Melted wax creased and flexed, fresh pools of it dripping in slow, agonizing drops off her skin and onto the floor.

Her hollow eye sockets bore into him, the empty caverns desolate and full of anger, mouth falling until it touched the point of her jawline, curling into a snarl. Her face twitched, and another chunk of wax, flaking from her cheek, sank to the ground. The crow cocked his head as she raised her fingers to scratch at the place it fell from, digging her long, curled nails into her skin, until her first digit plunged so deep inside, she couldn't remove it. Mayhem cringed as Harrow pulled her fingers from the folds of her face, leaving several large, dimpled cavities in their wake.

"They're trying to leave again, aren't they?"

She moaned a tortured cry; her face contorted into a horrific scream that echoed off the walls, bouncing from the floorboards to the ceiling. It encased them both, ringing so loudly that Mayhem jumped from his place atop her cage, his wings flapping aggressively, exhausted from the effort it took to keep him afloat.

It *had* been quiet inside of the house on the hill, and the children must have known she would come for them soon. They were young, but they were not stupid enough to believe that their dreams of a quiet house would last.

Quiet gave Harrow time to plot, time to prepare for them, to feel and to breathe and to hurt. It didn't mean that the children would finally escape, or that they would be free. Quiet meant, for Harrow, it was time to play.

The children were doomed, no matter how long she dragged it out.

She now stood directly in front of her mirror, the only object in the room left whole and unbroken. It was dirty, not cleaned for what looked like decades, but as her mouth hung open, the blacks of her eye sockets staring directly into its depths, time seemed to stop.

It was as if the woman made of wax was seeing herself for the first time. Her fingers grazed the sides of her face—though not penetrating the skin like before—fresh flames dancing against her hardened exterior. Her fire was never fully extinguished. As much as she tried to smother them, they would always return eventually. She leaned closer to the mirror, inspecting every inch of what she had become, voids holed into her face beneath her brows.

"Some days, I think it's my face that keeps them away from me."

Mayhem watched as she pinched and pulled at her skin, tearing bits of it off. Each flake fell to the floor, disappearing into the carpet. He wasn't sure if she waited for a response.

The crow, exhausted, dropped to the floor, the black of his feathers masked within the shadows cast from her open window.

"Mayhem, we've been friends a long time. You would tell me if it was my face that bothered them, right?"

There was that word again, "friend". The sound of it

grated against his bones. Harrow had chosen her form, reveled in the terror her face caused after years of carving and shaping it. Everything Harrow did was intentional. Seeing her so unsure rattled him. Harrow was nothing if not drenched in conviction. Maybe, if she melted away from existence, if she too was bored and tired of her games, they would all finally be free.

The crow was the only living being able to see her and remain alive in this room. He was the only one she spoke to, the only one she asked questions of. He was the first to see the horrors that happened behind this door, and he was the only one able to see this part of her, too.

Such was his burden to carry.

The few moments of hushed silence killed what was left of his optimism. Harrow stomped her foot, swinging to face him suddenly, with rage coating each slippery feature.

"You don't know what you're talking about, *bird*." The insult spat from her lips. It hung in the air between them as if he had challenged her. Mayhem jumped, escaping to her high standing wardrobe, deeper within the room. Harrow's cruel scowl followed him as he moved, but the wood already felt more stable beneath each talon.

She made the effort of taking a hazardous step towards him, but apparently rethought her next move, turning back to the mirror instead. Harrow said nothing after that for a long while, insistent on keeping their truce of solitude, of quiet friendship.

This was their game, the dance they gifted to each other, hot and cold, predator and prey. It never changed. Mayhem wasn't sure if either of them could do this for much longer.

Harrow itched to choose another victim. Mayhem could sense it. She found joy in listening to the walls and slinking into the shadows to find them. Her hands would tremble with excitement before entering the dark, her fingers flexing, spraying wax in thick droplets as the digits stretched in anticipation.

The crow couldn't remember how many children survived in the house presently, but it was enough. She would pick a child from the pack and bring them back to her lair before her game of all games began.

His gaze drifted from the crone back to the gilded cage she kept open for him. Sometimes, it felt like a punishment. She was so desperate for companionship, and each refusal Mayhem delivered was another dagger into the heart of a child.

Because, if it wasn't him, it was one of them, and Mayhem was nothing but self-serving. He would not give himself over to her willingly, not even to save the children from their cruel fates.

Harrow kept them trapped as pets here, just as she would Mayhem, if he allowed it. At first, all would be well; she would care for them for several days, feeding them scraps of what she pulled from her hollow, giving them everything she was capable of giving. Soon after, when the thrill of the chase had lost its luster, when the child had proven to not fill the vacant hole in her perforated heart, was when Harrow's true form came to play.

Far crueler, and far deadlier.

She would rip them, limb by limb, leaving them to suffer against the metal floor of their kennel. Smeared blood stained the metal coop, and dried strings of entrails littered the outside, like decorative pot-pourri, stinking of rot. Harrow would hurt them so badly that they did more than just die in her care. They were marred to the point of indistinguishability. It was as if they never existed at all.

Harrow's body suffocated them as she held them, and when their bodies melted into hers, when she devoured them whole and spat out the bones, she would cry until the sun rose.

Over time, Mayhem had realized her sad truth—she only ever wanted to be loved.

But love desired nothing of the hag of wax.

Chapter 4
The Rat

"I saw a door with no handle, I'm telling you!"

Blue was adamant that she'd seen it once, but not even Flea believed her. He knew how easy it was for the maze to play tricks on them.

Her hushed whispers turned furious, and the girl spoke so quickly that he could not understand her through her frustration. The group stared at her in concern, but by the looks in their eyes, they had already dismissed her belief.

Flea lay curled up in the center of the circle of children, though they had moved themselves a few hours ago. They'd been arguing since they got here, but were at least relatively safe for another night.

Moving kept them alive.

This human space was smaller than the last, but that wasn't a terrible stroke of luck. A smaller space meant that they could keep an easy eye on every corner. The wax woman could slip between the cracks in the walls, she could travel through the maze in ways they couldn't begin to understand. Flea felt less tense in the space they had acquired for the night.

"That isn't the great news you think it is." Greasy grumbled, to Flea's right. Flea turned his head to face him, whiskers twitching in amusement. Out of all of them, Flea thought Greasy looked the oldest, but age was so hard to tell with humans.

Everyone here was unnaturally thin, but it wasn't due to age. Their skin didn't sag or wrinkle like his mother's had, and they didn't limp or move like their joints were brittle and breaking. Instead, the children moved with the vitality of newborn pups, with skin porcelain smooth like the wet tip of his snout. It was a mystery to Flea how they grew older, with so little signs of wear and tear.

It happened so rarely here in the maze.

Harrow didn't discriminate when she took them to her lair. Old, young, poor or rich, the flesh must have tasted the same for her to keep coming for them the way she did.

Despite his age, the boy's mannerisms marked him as the naivest of the group. He snorted and mocked, exuding an arrogance that set Flea's whiskers on edge.

"But it's a *door*." Blue said again, more impatient this time.

"We walk through about twelve of them a day," Greasy argued. Amongst the children, there was a distinct divide; several of them nodded their heads in agreement. Others looked at the girl with wide, but trusting, eyes.

Blue had been in the maze the longest, and it pulled a lot of weight with the impressionable crowd. She didn't look like the type to lead a revolution, but she was clear-headed and quick on her feet. She knew how to survive in the labyrinth.

"I think we could find it again... I think it might be the way out of here, for good."

Flea lifted his tail and let it drop with a heavy thud. He

was inclined to trust Blue mostly—his life was partially due to her wit—but this, this door with no handle, felt far-fetched. The children's gazes sank, their hopes soured. The longer she talked, the deeper the hole she dug herself into.

When Blue finally fell silent, Flea glanced at Greasy again. He played with his fingers, picking at the now bleeding skin of a nail bed.

"You can't open a handle-less door." He whispered, a small shake in his voice.

This was no victory. The boy had not wished to be right. He didn't want to undermine Blue, Flea realized, rather, he hoped she could prove him wrong.

And Blue's conviction wasn't strong enough to convince him.

Flea stood on his tired pink paws, claws scraping against the floor, and sidled closer to the eldest. His warm body melted into the boy's thigh, causing a shiver to rumble through his tiny frame. He could offer no assurances. But understanding, comfort, and companionship, those he had aplenty.

Blue's eyes bore into the rat. He felt her sense of betrayal hot against his back. But Flea didn't belong to Blue. He didn't belong to any of them.

He only belonged to the maze.

"You're an idiot." She removed her heavy gaze from Flea's back and returned to her aggressor. Tired frustration simmered her words. "*Any* door can be opened. We haven't tried it yet! It's so different from all the others, it has to be the one."

Greasy opened his mouth to speak, but Bear beat him to it.

"What makes you think we can actually escape?"

"I don't *know*," she sounded exasperated, but there was

31

still a fight in her. "We walked into this house. That means there must be a way out."

"I haven't believed that since we lost the last three kids."

The silence was so deafening it hurt. Flea didn't know who needed his comfort more. Fresh tears fell from faces to the floor. Noses sniffled.

Flea's body trembled as he felt the boy's hand resting on his back. Each stroke of the warm paw smoothed the thin layer of oil on Flea's fur, a silent gesture of solidarity that eased his uncertainty. The rat lifted his paws to lick the pink skin before rubbing them over his face, picking at the dried wax between his toenails and flinging the remnants toward the carcass film on the ground.

"I still think it's smarter to move again. It's been quiet in the house, and *she's* bound to come crawling around soon. Wouldn't be surprised if it was tonight."

Despite the doubts and the shadows of past losses that loomed over them, Blue's eyes remained dry. They narrowed at Greasy and Bear, her determination unwavering. Flea watched as her fingers flexed into small fists.

"If she comes for us tonight, we can't let her take another one. We can't keep running forever."

The boy opened his mouth to argue, but Flea pressed his body to his hand again to give him pause.

Blue turned to the others, her gaze sweeping over each face in the dim light of their hiding place. "I know it's scary. I know we've lost so much already. But we have to try."

The weight of their situation pressed upon him, air thickened with its tang, and Flea's fur bristled with worry. He turned his head to quickly lick down the rising hairs.

"I'm sorry," the small girl to Blue's left said, wrapping her tender fingers around Blue's arm. Smalls was the only half appropriate name for her that Flea could come up with.

"I think you're right. You both are. We need to escape, and maybe you *did* see the door. Maybe that was the right one. But we're too tired for it now. Let's cross the hallways again, find a space for the night, and take a stab at it tomorrow."

"We shouldn't move; this room is perfect." Greasy quickly interjected. "It takes everything just to try to cross the hallways without making a sound. Especially with all of us. Why can't we stay?"

"Harrow is most active when it's quiet," Smalls frowned at him. Flea could taste the memory of the last child he'd watched the Hag snatch, on a night similar to this, "I know you're tired, but while we're moving, the house knows we're playing the game. The walls will tell her where we're at if it gets bored, you know that as well as I do. We've seen it happen."

Blue huffed, crossing her arms over her chest. As if to punctuate Small's words, the walls inhaled, pulling inward before mirroring Blue's breath by swelling outward.

Everyone froze.

Just outside the door, something being dragged along the floor rent the air with how near it felt.

Panic flickered into six pairs of eyes as all their heads swung toward the door, their hearts in their mouths, as a blanket of cold descended over them.

"We go. Now," Blue insisted, her wide eyes locking with Flea's. "There's no time."

They moved. Blue's hand snaked along the floor. Beckoned Flea towards her. He sprinted up her arm and curled his tail around her neck for support as she rose.

The children trembled, a silent agreement, a commitment passing between them as they hardened themselves to fight.

Skkrrrrrrrittttttt Skrrrrrritttt Skritttttt

Blue led. They crept towards the door, their footsteps muffled by the thick wood. Flea clung tightly to Blue's shoulder, his tiny heart racing in time with hers.

As Blue reached out for the doorknob, her hand froze mid-air. The door *creeaakked* open on its own, to a darkened corridor beyond. A cold draft swept into the room, the faint scent of musk drifting along it.

"Move," Blue whispered, her voice barely audible over her pounding heart; Flea's ear pressed close to her throat. Without a glance at the group huddled behind her, she stepped over the threshold and into the unknown. Flea heard the others follow, their fear thick on his whiskers, leaving behind the safety of the known for the uncertainty of the maze.

There was no going *back*. It might not exist should they turn to find it.

The corridor stretched before them, shadows dancing in the dim light. Flea's grip tightened on her shoulder and his tail lashed back and forth uncontrollably as his body shook, while they ventured further into the labyrinth. Their faint footsteps sank into the tension that hung in the air.

The walls closed in.

Funneled forward, their gazes darted from side to side, waiting for Harrow to unfurl from every shadow.

Blue halted abruptly, causing the others to stumble to a stop behind her. She raised a hand for quiet, her eyes narrowing as she listened intently.

To the silence.

"She's hunting."

Flea's ears pricked. The faintest scratch could be made

out behind the walls, but only to his rodent ears. Every few feet, the sound registered, causing him to flinch as it scraped against the beams beneath the wallpaper. Blue's head snapped to the side behind them, and Flea instinctively mirrored her movement. He fought to keep focus on the unsettling echoes within the walls, a rising dread coiling in his chest, convinced that if he looked away for even a moment, Harrow would break through.

But behind them came another threat.

Blue gasped as the hallway behind her twisted and elongated into a shadowy obscurity. Smalls stumbled, her small figure fading into the distance, the space between her and the children stretching like a dark abyss. With each passing second, the child seemed to shrink, silently screaming as the hall took her further away, each note swallowed by the insatiable darkness that pulled her from them.

"Grab Pia!" Blue's echoing command sliced through the tension.

Flea watched in horror as the nearest child thrust out their arm. It extended so far, the rat was sure it would break, but it held. Smalls gripped the outstretched, elongated hand tightly, her screams reverberating as the walls threatened to close in around her. Her body hung, pitched forward, one foot pinned to the ground while the other drifted in the air.

With a frantic heave, they pulled her forward; the effort sending the group of children tumbling to the floor as the corridor snapped back to its usual shape.

Smalls lay, shaking, her breaths taken in shuddering, frantic gasps.

"I was screaming," she stammered, eyes wide with terror. "It felt like no matter how hard I tried, I couldn't get any closer to you guys. And I swear, something kept trying to *grab* my ankles."

The weight of the moment settled on Flea's shoulders, a gnawing hopelessness taking root in his bones. Blue stood frozen, heavy breaths escaping her, as tears streamed down Small's cheeks.

She glanced at Flea, then towards her friends, the flickering light in her eyes fading.

The labyrinth had a will of its own and would always serve its master. One of them would be left behind. Flea saw it each time they tried to move. He watched time and time again as the maze played with its victims, delivering them all on a silver platter for Harrow, while he escaped into the floorboards.

"Go on without me," Blue whispered, waving her hands for the children to disperse behind her, while her gaze seemed lost, far away, unfocused. They looked at her incredulously. Her mouth thinned, her head snapping up to stare at them.

"Seriously, *go!*"

"We can't leave you," Lanky Boy whispered. "Without you, where will we go?"

"Alaric, if I can't go back home, I'm going to die trying. You guys might want to find another room for the night. But I *won't die here*. I'm not looking for another room to hide in. I'm finding that door."

Her face was hard, lines of determination etched deep between her brows, her expression set in stubborn resolve.

"She'll take you, like she tried with Pia!"

"Hold on to each other," Blue ignored the newest boy. "You have to hurry. The house won't try to separate you if I go off alone. Find a place to hide. I promise I'll come back for you, with help, when I get out."

Baaaannngg!

The rumble began as a low, resonant growl, rolling through the air like distant thunder. It swelled gradually, vibrating the floorboards beneath their feet, echoing off the walls with a haunting, hollow timbre that felt alive.

"Go!" Blue demanded, wrapping slender fingers around Flea, making sure his claws were clenched deep into her shirt before she moved. "Find a safe room. Don't let her get you tonight."

Flea felt her shoulders straighten, and she removed her grip from his back, her hands curling into fists at her sides. With a final nod to the others, she turned and ran down the corridor before they could argue further.

He wasn't surprised when the hallway tightened around them, and when he turned back to look at the children they had abandoned, they were already gone.

Flea's small form trembled on Blue's shoulder, his keen senses picking up on every subtle movement and sound around them as they navigated the labyrinthine passages of the maze.

"Thank you for coming with me, Flea," Blue whispered, raising her hand to curl her finger around his fleshy tale. The rat's nose twitched in response. As if he had a choice.

She was brave. But doomed.

And he wouldn't go down with her.

Chapter 5
The Crow

Upon arrival, Mayhem anticipated his return to the house on the hill would be punctuated by the cries of a child freshly tossed into their death cage. When he'd flown around the house several times, worried he had arrived too late, an uncomfortable, eerie silence stretched across the property.

He circled a few times too many, prolonging the inevitable moment when he would discover Harrow's victim's face, whichever child it was this time around. Their screams, their pleas for help...the crow could not bear the guilt of their deaths for much longer.

When Mayhem reached the highest windowsill and hovered a few inches above the wood, his beaded black eyes turned toward the gilded cage that always stood primed for him.

His beak opened in a long, deep sigh of relief as he landed, his three toes at the front of each foot digging into the sill, his back toes anchoring him straight. The door on the bird cage swung on its hinges, back and forth, its movement mimicking his wings, almost ethereal in its laziness. It creaked into the silence, slicing the calm with the ease of a knife through butter.

The crow hopped from the ledge and into the room.

Usually, she would be here. There were very few places Harrow could be when she wasn't trapping herself within the confines of her own room. Mayhem hopped from the sill to the dresser to the floor, the feel of hardened wax flooding the space between each talon. His claws dug deep into the carpet, coming up with flaking grime and rot.

He very rarely ventured this deep into her lair. Only when Harrow was out of sight, on the hunt through her home for another victim, did Mayhem dare to let himself be so exposed. His back was to the window, the cage and her accompanied wardrobe stood directly to his right.

He looked around and took hesitant, heavy steps throughout the room. Each time his foot connected with the old, glazed carpet, his claws sank deep; with every step, he met resistance; like he was in a pit of waxy quicksand.

Mayhem felt drawn onward, deeper into her lair. His inquisitive nature betrayed him, demanding he push his self-imposed boundary. His head jerked side to side, every feather held brittle against his body, awaiting the moment she would pounce; the crow lured on by the unsettling desire to torture himself, it seemed.

The light from his window bounced off Harrow's mirror, casting fragmented reflections that pranced like phantoms on the floor, the flickering shadows from the wardrobe twisting and warping, each movement pricking at his instincts.

He continued forward unsteadily, drunk on the unease of being so far inside the hell house. The air felt *off*, not quite as empty as it looked without Harrow here. Her room was still somber, sickening, sticky with her rotted presence. It paralyzed the crow.

It was as if she hadn't really left at all...

A movement...

Harrow's hands emerged from the shadow cast by the wardrobe, ghostly, as if the darkness itself had coalesced to reach for him, her fingers stretching like tendrils of smoke. The moment she grazed his feathers, the very essence of the shadows had come alive, hungry to drag him into the depths of her grip.

The crow's heart seized, his breathing caught, and his wings flapped in panic. Harrow held on with both hands, candle fingertips wrapping tightly around his chest. Though he could not see her face yet, her voice rose from under the wax, submerged in her molt.

"You thought I couldn't get you, bird. Oh...but I have proved you wrong."

Each word dripped with sinister delight, wrapping around him like a vice. Mayhem squirmed, heart racing, his instincts screaming for flight, but Harrow's grip tightened, anchoring him in place. The warmth of her touch contrasted sharply with the chill creeping into his bones, and he felt the weight of her intent pressing down, suffocating and inescapable.

Mayhem thrashed, tried to squawk, but nothing would come out. Her grip was so tight against him, her fingers suffocating the life and sound and all that he was from his body. His chest constricted, ribs bowing inward until the sharp grinding of bone against bone nearly broke him. Every breath became a fight, his lungs unable to fully expand, crushed beneath the weight of her fingers digging mercilessly into his sides. Writhing in agony, his ribcage no longer a protective cage but a trap, squeezing tighter with each second, threatening to snap entirely, and then—*crack*.

His hollow bones, fragile and delicate, fractured under the pressure, sharp pangs of torture ripping through him. His entire body had begun to splinter apart, piece by piece, crumbling like dried branches.

One jagged bone splintered and sliced through his thin membranous skin, piercing through the surface like a shard of glass. It jutted out, glistening in the faint light, the edges slick with blood as it protruded grotesquely from his wing. The sight as horrific as the sensation, the once smooth feathered limb now broken and bleeding, an alien thing, twisted beyond recognition.

With a slow, deliberate motion, Harrow pulled herself from the shadow, rising as if she were being drawn up from the depths of the floor itself. Her form emerged in a grotesque ballet, limbs contorting unnaturally, the darkness clinging to her like a second skin. Every inch of her body unfolded with a chilling fluidity, her elbows pushing through the film of wax to gain purchase as she pushed herself up and her knees appeared, her body slow and sinuous as a cat.

A grin stretched across the hag's face, cracking the seams like shattered glass. Her hardened exterior slipped away, tendrils of long milky white wax rolling down her jawline to reveal fresh new skin underneath, soft and delicate, like the petals of a freshly bloomed flower glorying in the radiance of his pain.

Part of her face looked velvet to the touch, a glimpsed weakness, the softness that hid underneath all the ugly melting parts of her. Wax rolled down her cheeks in waves, her face slipping until it layered incomprehensibly, once again hiding her inner softness behind a newly varnished shell.

Until she was Harrow once more.

She turned her malignant eyeless gaze towards his black eyes, panic flitting from one iris to the other while he pushed against her in determination.

Her fingers ignited at the tips.

Flames threatened to engulf him. Mayhem blinked, and her fire tickled his feathers. Until it charred him. Until her hands crushed him.

Until it felt like the end of him.

Until suddenly, it was gone.

"My sweet Mayhem, you didn't think I would let you die that easily, did you?"

Harrow dragged the wicks against his scalding plumage and the bird choked back a gargled cry. She let go of him then, fresh steam wafting from each digit as she loosened her hands from around his body.

Relief flushed through him as he dropped like a rock, to smack into the ground like dead, steaming meat. Mayhem staggered upright, hobbled a few steps, unable to move his wings, which sagged, twisted, shattered, from her attempt to break him.

"Your clipped wings will heal. Eventually," her voice caressed him, her face remaining close behind him as he stumbled forward, "but you will not leave me. You, Mayhem, can never leave me."

The crow's vision blurred, but he was determined to focus on her face again. He couldn't keep his eyes off of her, he had learned that, and he hated himself for that dependence. In his time in the house on the hill, that was the first lesson he ever taught himself.

And he had failed.

Harrow crouched on all fours behind him. Turning around, torturously, slowly, his wings dragging behind him, Mayhem saw her chin nestled safely in the crooks of her propped palms. A languorous smile leered down at him.

"Tell me why they want to leave me." She whispered softly, closing her lids over her hollowed sockets. Her mouth twitched, drool forming at the corners of her mouth.

Mayhem hobbled just out of reach, his back now flush against one of the walls furthest from the window. *His* window. On the floor, red brush strokes trailed to the tips of his wings, his feather tips sticky with his own blood.

There was no helping a woman as lonely as Harrow. She continued, unconcerned by his silence, making up his responses as she saw fit in her own mind.

"I know you venture into town and listen to the whispers of the people below our hill. I know they speak ill of me. Tell me, Mayhem, what do they say?"

He would never tell her the truth.

Everyone felt the house's presence, lurking like a storm cloud over their lives. The windows blackened and broken; the porch sagging under the weight of its own gloom.

Her house was haunted. Condemned.

They said anyone who ventured too close would feel a chill creep into their bones, as if the house itself exhaled a cold breath. Those who walked the narrow trail that wound past it would sprint, hearts pounding, as if the very act of looking at it could curse them with misfortune.

Years went by, and the stories grew taller. Parents, once bold enough to dismiss the tales as mere children's fancies, began to worry. Each time they recounted the tales, their voices grew quieter, laced with an unsettling truth that made them shiver. They began to believe it themselves.

And the missing children? Who searches for waifs when they were never cared for to begin with?

Harrow looked for those that were left to fend for themselves and offered the vision of home to those that could not live safely with their own family. Perhaps that's why those stories had faded from conversation; the townsfolk were reluctant to confront the reality of what they had allowed to happen to their own children.

"I was their candle flame, Mayhem." Harrow's voice filled the room, ancient and all knowing. She was the demon that feasted on children, the witch that loved to play games. The beldam that spun golden threads into her web, patiently waiting until the flies ensnared themselves.

"I'm sure it looks much different now than before. It's been so many years, Mayhem, since I walked the meadows that surrounded the town. But it was beautiful. Flowers bloomed no matter the season, and traders traveled from afar just to glimpse the magic they found here."

Mayhem didn't care. His wings had begun to scream. Lances of white-hot pain from his burnt flesh crawled up his neck. The breeze brushed the bone fragment protruding from his wing. Smoke rose from his still smoldering feathers. She did not speak of a world he knew.

The world was not beautiful. The forest's foliage spoiled by rot and decay; Mayhem hadn't even known that meadows existed nearby. What was left from her time of magic was nothing but dead expanses of land. It went on for miles, lost amongst hills, and the passage of time.

"I must admit, I was allured by the magic here, too. Like called to like."

Then she came, drifting in from whatever hell had birthed her, settling like a parasite in the heart of it. She fed on the land's magic, drinking it dry like a tick, sinking her claws into its bones until nothing remained but ruin. The crops withered, the rivers darkened, and the people—those who hadn't fled—became hollow-eyed husks. Even now, as the last ember of life flickered in the streets, she lingered, waiting, watching. Because love can be cruel when it refuses to let go.

Harrow sat up on her shins, her joints cracking as Mayhem shivered and pressed further into the shadows. If he backed up any more, he would be swallowed by the tearing wallpaper completely. The crow lifted his beak to taste the stale air around them. His heart beat rapidly, his panic not subsiding, even with the sweet tempo of Harrow's voice.

The Hag might be lying, and he would never know.

Still, the lies that inevitably escaped her somehow entranced Mayhem. It was a different kind of trap, the kind that he fell into willingly. Even with his broken wings and his crushed rib cage, he couldn't help but close his eyes.

"You should have seen them, Mayhem," she sighed, tilting her head as the crow ruffled his feathers. "The villagers, after I drained the last drop of magic from this place. They just... stood there. Empty. Hollow-eyed. Nothing left inside but the shape of what they used to be."

Harrow moved about the room, gliding across the floor, back to her usual pacing. She appeared lost in her own story, and the crow with her. Hobbled, broken, what more could he do?

She traced a slow circle on a dust-covered table, her voice dripping with amusement. "It was inspiring, really. The way their mouths hung open like they wanted to speak but had forgotten how. The way their limbs moved just a second too late, like they weren't quite real anymore. Such a tragedy, don't you think?"

Mayhem let out a sharp croak, and she laughed, soft and knowing. "Oh, don't look at me like that. I couldn't let all that go to waste. I needed something for the children. They'll be scared at first, of course. They always are. But they'll settle in faster if they have something familiar."

Harrow's waxen skin glistened with a sheen that belied the rot lurking beneath. The corners of her mouth curled into a twisted sneer, a brief crack in her eerie façade that revealed the darkness within. Even as she reminisced, a twitch flickered in her hollow socket—an unsettling reminder that beneath the stillness lay a restless soul, twisted by years of neglect and fury. She was a specter of both comfort and fear, and no amount of wax could conceal the sinister warmth of her twisted compassion.

She leaned forward, eye sockets glinting in the dim light. "So, I made them something. A new toy. Something close to human, as close as I could get. I molded the limbs just right, set the heads at the proper tilt, shaped the smiles so they stretched just far enough. The eyes were the hardest part—you know how important the eyes are." She sighed, running a finger beneath Mayhem's beak. "They're not perfect, not yet. More like me than them, but I tried. I really did. The children should feel safe, after all. They should think they're among friends. Maybe then they won't leave me."

Her smile curled, sharp and cruel. "And when they finally notice what's wrong, when they hear the way those familiar voices scrape and crack, when those almost-human hands reach just a little too far—" she exhaled, eyes closing as if savoring the thought, "—oh, it will be too late, won't it?"

Mayhem shifted, claws tightening on the wood.

She laughed, low and pleased. "Yes, bird. Let's see how long they last."

Mayhem's tail feathers twitched into the silence of her absent words when she stopped talking. He opened his eyes, unaware that he had them clenched tight against the pain. The woman made of wax stood in front of her mirror again, her toes melting into the carpet. He couldn't see what held her attention, but she looked so lost in it that it didn't seem to matter. She was in a world far beyond here.

"Is that too far? I know I go too far sometimes."

She always loved them too much, loved them too hard, in her own way. Harrow crushed everything in her embrace, holding it so tightly that the objects of her affections saw nothing but six feet of earth at the end of their lives.

Mayhem could hear the pain that nestled between each syllable, how heartache drove her to near insanity. A monster that hunted for love, for an acceptance she would never receive in return.

"Pay attention, Mayhem. This is important."

As if he could take his eyes off her—as if the crow would *ever* let Harrow out of his sight again. His wings ached, his broken bones shaking with each beat of his heart.

"I've always wanted children of my own. But we monsters don't get that luxury, bird. You know that, don't you?"

He pressed his back further against the shadowed walls, wishing he could sink into them. It might have been easier that way, to become a part of the home that he couldn't seem to stay away from.

"When I started collecting the children, I made sure they wanted me. I didn't just pluck them from homes because it amused me." Mayhem watched as her face furrowed, as if he had been the one to accuse her of the atrocity. "They were lost and broken. Unwanted and unloved. I'm *trying*."

"But. They keep. Trying. To. Leave. ME!"

Her screech was a mixture of sorrow and anger. Worse than frustration, a rage that was so deep within her it echoed through the house. Everything shook; the house shuddered as if struck, moving around them in anxious ripples, expanding away from her like it wanted to flee. Mayhem felt the wallpaper bubble behind him, could hear the hallways shifting and changing beyond the door, minimizing access to her wrath.

As if the house was just as afraid of Harrow as the rest of them.

Harrow planted her feet on the ground and curled her hands into tight fists. Her lips opened in a vicious sneer, melted wax dripping onto her tongue, stark white fangs protruding from the top and bottom of her cavernous mouth. Her jaw extended amid her howl, opening so much, her chin almost came to a crashing halt on the floor.

Teeth elongated to points, sharp as a wolf's. They would have pierced the floor had she bitten down. Drool slid upon each ivory tusk, the last remnants of her scream flicking each drop, to splatter across the floor in front of the crow.

It ended mere minutes later, Mayhem drenched in sweat and slobber and fear. Harrow moved again. Snorting. Animal. Lost in her hunger. Quicker than he'd seen her before, moving with purpose instead of her gentle pacing. The crow flinched as she approached him, unable to flee, craning his head to stare up at her as she loomed over him. The gilded cage on the other side of the room glinted, almost beckoning him, but then the ghost of her fingers wrapped around his fragile frame and gently *pushed* him down. He shrank until his face was pressed deep into the wax encrusted floor. Broken. Trapped. He would become nothing but a haunting memory in the house on the hill, much like the children that died in the birdcage before him.

Harrow did not stop in front of the crow. She didn't stop until she was at her closed door instead, leaving Mayhem and the mirror, and the tired open cage. The woman of wax turned to face him, her jaw shrinking just enough that it wouldn't be a nuisance as she crawled through her home.

Her hollow eyes burnt. Pits of darkness, soaking in all the light from the room and casting gloom instead. Beak fixed, tipped into the air, Mayhem saw the moment Harrow scented what lay just beyond the door, like a hound caught on a trail.

Her entire body stiffened. Like a dog. An angry, violent predator.

She sniffed until she was satisfied. Mayhem caught it. The slightest hint of fear, the smell of crusted grime, layered on cotton shirts and the faintest tang of sweat that stained under their arms.

The children were on the move.

They couldn't know how terrible their timing was, hadn't seen what Mayhem witnessed in the last hour, in what might become his tomb. If they had, they would have known better. They wouldn't be moving, wouldn't be scheming. They would have been safe in their hiding spot, at least for a little while longer.

Harrow snapped out of her trance, her wicked fingers hungrily reaching for the doorknob. It twisted before she touched it; the house bending to her will, eager to appease. Magic flickered around her.

Mayhem clicked his beak wordlessly. No sound would be enough to warn them of her imminent arrival. She would find them like she always did, and Mayhem wouldn't be able to escape it this time. He could already feel the wax molding around him, flowing towards the crow, slow but steady. Soon it would encase him, much like the cage he had avoided for so long.

He would have to watch as she tortured one, encased in his waxy prison. His eyes forced wide open; his broken form cemented into an unyielding position. The guilt that had chased him for so long would finally catch up with him.

The door opened before her, a breeze snaking into the room like a tomb opened for the first time. The once stale air that settled in the hallway rippled with darkened magic.

Mayhem opened his beak once more, his desperate attempt to warn the children failing as the wax crawled up his feathered chest. He shut his mouth before it could infiltrate his throat and fill his lungs.

Harrow crawled out the door, along the walls, into the creases where the ceiling joined them, the *skritt skritt* of her nails skittering along their surfaces the only sound. She disappeared from sight, out, into the hellmouth of her home, ready to pluck the next child for their gruesome end.

Chapter 6
The Rat

Flea couldn't keep Blue safe, and the girl in her starving, drained state, could not offer him protection, either.

He fidgeted along her shoulder, clinging onto her with his sharpened claws. She winced as his talons dug into her flesh each time she shifted. Blue stuck to the shadows, and even though she moved slowly and silently, the movement jostled Flea so much that he had a hard time keeping himself upright. His tail began to hurt from the strain of remaining erect, the cost of lending him balance.

"I never liked the quiet," she hissed at him, whispering so low that he could hardly hear her.

He couldn't agree. Flea preferred silence. He needed to stay vigilant and kept his ears to the ground. It was the only way he had remained alive for as long as he had.

Sooner or later, this girl would die. That was clear, as she continued talking, filling up the space in the halls with the hushed, worried whispers of her fear. He wanted to tell her to be quiet, his claws gripped tightly onto her shoulder in warning, but she couldn't understand him.

"I was always the loudest in the room," she continued,

unaware of how even her whispers echoed off the walls. She fingered the wallpaper, dragging her index against the torn bits of paper, leaving raw, exposed wood underneath. It could have splintered, but she wouldn't have noticed. Blue was in a world of her own.

"We didn't have much, and I didn't understand what that meant at the time, I just talked about what I thought I wanted and needed. I think my momma hated me because of it." Blue kicked some of the dust layered below her feet. "I'm just a kid, though. How was I supposed to know that they couldn't afford to feed me anymore?

"Mum's not looking for me. Or my daddy. I think they let me come here, knowing I wouldn't ever come home." Flea shifted uncomfortably on her shoulder, his tiny talons gripping a little too tightly. His tail flicked back and forth in agitation, the weight of their conversation making it impossible for him to stay still.

Every few seconds, he readjusted his position, claws scraping lightly against her, eyes darting around nervously. The hair on his back stood on end, betraying the unease he tried to hide.

Her story was not unique. Flea heard his fair share of horror stories from the children that were welcomed inside the maze on the hill. Each narrative was similar by design. Harrow only preyed on cast-offs who had nothing left.

She brought her plague to their town, and they fell right into her trap.

"When daddy said we were going for a walk, and momma was crying, I should have figured it out. I was a big mouth to feed. That was all. They were happy when I ran off. Daddy encouraged it."

She kept talking, and Flea wanted her to stop. He thought about biting her, but believing Harrow was hunting made him hesitate. His claws gripped around her even tighter, his whiskers twitching uncomfortably. He didn't want to know any more about her; didn't want to care. It would make it that much harder to watch when Harrow inevitably took her, like she took everyone.

"I don't even think he yelled for me when I was too far ahead. He watched me go and just turned back around."

It was the last straw.

"You're hurting me," Blue whispered, reaching her hand to grab him from her shoulder. Flea resisted the urge to gnaw at her flesh, quickly shuffling his weight across her neck to avoid her reach. He squeaked incoherently.

"Follow me closely. I promise I won't leave you."

She still didn't understand how frustrated he was. The rat frowned. His nose twitched defiantly, wanting to drill his teeth deep into her skin, but he resisted. She knelt, arm outstretched to the floor, her hand placed flat like a step. Slowly, Flea traveled down Blue's arm, trying hard to not injure her further with his claws.

When his paws reached the stable floor again, the rat scurried quickly into the darkness.

"Wait! Where are you going?"

Flea abandoned her, pressing so deep into the walls that he could have sunk into them. He knew Blue couldn't see him, not when the lanterns that flickered in the hallway lit only a foot in either direction. Not enough for her to catch his sandy fur as it moved against the wood.

"Flea!" she sobbed. Blue's voice rose to a dangerous level, one that would soak into the walls and leak into Harrow's quarters. The Hag would be moving soon, slipping between the cracks in the wallpaper, creeping along her tunnels and passages that only she knew how to navigate.

He felt sorry for Blue; knew he was leaving her to her death. He felt for the girl, she who he had gone through so much with, but Flea needed to leave. He couldn't turn back now; he couldn't save her. He needed to erase her memory and the pain that would follow.

Maybe she would survive.

He had scampered so far down the hallway that he lost her completely. Even the sound of her cries receded now that the walls moved around him, and the rooms shifted. Flea didn't slip through any cracks or holes, didn't cross any doors or thresholds, but when he looked back for Blue, the walls had moved and there was nothing left of her to be seen. Swallowed by the maze like the others.

She was on her own.

A pool of guilt dropped into the depths of Flea's belly, like a stone in his gut, swinging from side to side with each step he took. Despite his best efforts, it wouldn't subside. He hadn't asked to be attached, hadn't wanted to know the brave girl with the blue eyes as she entered his life. At all.

Memories were senseless. Stupid.

Attached or not, death caught everyone in the maze. Flea hated his time alone, yet company, for long, was deadly. Whether he was nestled inside his circle of children or slinking along the floorboards alone, Harrow could find them all if she wanted.

She could sense fear, like she could taste their tears, as they soaked through the floor like a sponge. Although Flea was not her primary target, if the rat entered her line of sight, there wouldn't be any evidence left for the children to find.

She'd swallow him whole.

He kept moving, and the walls kept shifting.

And he tried to forget.

Chapter 7
The Crow

THE MINUTE HARROW LEFT THE ROOM, MAYHEM COULD NO longer hear her. The woman made of wax was as silent as she was deadly.

Encased in the layers and layers of wax that continued to crawl up his body at an achingly slow pace, it felt like it was alive, sluggish and lazy, even without the monster that shed it. It bent to her every whim, moving on its own accord, like the shifting walls beyond Harrow's room.

The ground moved beneath the crow; the wax drifting like a nomad through each thread of carpet. Mayhem strained against the suction that trapped him, but to no avail. It was almost worse than the threat of the golden cage still waiting within his sight; he almost wished he could die at the hands of Harrow instead. At least that would feel meaningful, purposeful.

It took mere minutes before the wax oozed up to his neck, his once beautiful feathers now stiff and unmovable, caked with hardening wax and pink blood, the smallest tuft of onyx peaking above the surface. He closed his eyes as he felt slow creeping tendrils crawling up the back of his head, cresting his rounded crown.

His feathers twitched painfully, but he was determined to only remember them unbroken.

Mayhem imagined his wings spread out to either side, hovering above the dull red brick that was so faded it was practically bone white. He wouldn't dare to lay a claw across the shattered, dark gray rooftop, whose tiles flaked off like molted scales. It was nothing more than a large, unappealing Victorian anymore. No longer lavish, no longer decadent.

It was just the hell house now, but this daydream was far more inviting than his reality.

Mayhem was practically fully encased, his outer eyelids glued open, inner eyelids flicking back and forth, cleaning the wax from his eyes. Transparent, they allowed him to see at least the blur that was the light of the room, seen from underneath the cast. What was left free of the wax, unencumbered and unglued, was his beak, through which he breathed in small gasps of air.

The small squeak of a hinge shook him out of his trance. His breaths softened, frantic to stay still.

Was she back already?

It wasn't Harrow. That much he could tell. Her stench was something rotten, years of decay sticking to her like spider webs. The steps that accompanied the screeching of the hinge were just as soft as hers, but it couldn't be her.

For a moment he stilled, awaiting Harrow's charred voice to gloat at his predicament once more.

But it never did.

What came was the softest, most vulnerable gasp, followed by steps that were heavy on the carcass encrusted floor. Mayhem wished he could have turned to follow the sounds of stifled sobs as someone—it must have been a child—rifled through Harrow's things. Candles fell, and papers fluttered around him. The child searched for something, but Mayhem wasn't sure what. They would not find a way out of here, if that was what they were looking for. Maybe a weapon, but that would be useless against the hag of wax. His perch atop the window was not the escape they would be looking for, unless, of course, that escape meant the back end of a six-foot ditch, dug just for them.

He tried to speak, opening his mouth just enough that it cracked the wax that covered his beak. Stale air greeted him, and Mayhem opened his beak wider and wider, until he could push the last of his remaining pockets of air from his lungs in a solitary *caw*.

He didn't think it was loud enough.

To his surprise, the rustling around him stopped. The crow feared the worst, worried that he missed his chance, and that the child would leave. But the sound of crunching steps turned into sliding knees against the carpet, inching closer and closer until it seemed that the child was practically on top of him.

Warm hands gripped either side of his waxy frame, nails scratching against the velvet-like coating. He cawed again, not realizing how full of anguish it was.

Small, delicate hands picked near his beak. Mayhem fought the urge to snap at the skin, knowing full well that this was his only chance at freedom. He closed his eyes and breathed in deeply, while piece after piece of chipped wax fell away from him. When the child realized that he was still breathing, still *alive*, they became more frantic in their efforts. Mayhem liked to think their efficiency was for his benefit, though he wouldn't fool himself. Harrow was bound to be back any second, and the child was wasting their time and effort, to free him, rather than free themselves.

They wouldn't be doing it if they knew that he had multiple opportunities to make a similar choice and hadn't.

"I'm sorry," a voice spoke with just the hint of a whisper. Mayhem wasn't sure what they were referring to until the sharp sting of a plucked feather made him scream in agony. The child wrapped their fingers around his beak to stifle the outcry, and Mayhem tried to spread his now freed wings and take off from the ground, when his feet collapsed on him from the overwhelming pain.

He had forgotten his wings were shattered beyond repair.

"She'll hear us. Please stop!" The voice was pleading now, as if they regretted their decision to free the crow instead of running in the other direction like they should have. Mayhem tried to take steady breaths and refocus, though the pulsating beat against his wings was impossible to ignore.

His eyes finally opened, squinting against the glaring brightness that surrounded them both.

A frail girl sat before him, sickened, with sunken-in cheeks from starvation. She looked at him with fearful worry, and brought a finger to her lips to quieten him.

He shook out his tail feathers and stepped away from the waxy remnants of his recent prison. From his periphery, the wax seemed to move away from him with slow reluctance. It inched back from where it came, retreating, perhaps until its master returned to nurture it. Mayhem kept it in the corner of his eyesight, knowing he could never let it out of his mind again. The wax was no longer an innocent sideliner. It was a player in Harrow's games.

"I... I couldn't watch you die because of her." The girl

started crying again, fresh tears welling and falling down her face. He looked at her, taking in her bright blue eyes, her fear nestled under each twitch and every expression. "Are you hurt?"

He didn't speak to her, but he blinked slowly, trying once again to move one of his wings, wincing from the sharp stab that lanced through him. The girl noticed, reaching towards him with both hands.

Mayhem jumped back instinctively, but the girl did not hurt him. She didn't move towards him or try to grab his wounded frame. Instead, she waited, worrying the bottom of her lip as her hands shook in front of her.

"Let me help you," she begged.

Mayhem didn't move. He wished he could, but his muscles wouldn't let him. They stood like that for several minutes, both wishing that trust was more easily earned than the hell house required it to be. Finally, he hobbled unsteadily toward her, claws wrapping tightly onto her fingers as he slowly lowered himself into her cupped hands. She tried not to wince at his rough grip, but he couldn't help but notice her eyes tighten at the corners. If only he could have as gentle a touch as she did.

Mayhem was afraid of falling from her hands and back into the wax as she lifted him to her eye level. He was broken, trapped without the use of his wings.

Mayhem was forced to trust her now.

"I'm sorry she hurt you."

The girl shouldn't be talking, she should be keeping her mouth clamped shut. This place wasn't like the rest, it wasn't just a furnished room left to gather dust over time. She had to know that this was Harrow's room. It was as if she couldn't see the trail of dried organs, or the blood stains splattered over the walls. Alone the smell...

She was so worried about Mayhem's rescue that it made her own survival impossible.

"I wish I had known before they sent me here that it would be this way. If I had known, maybe I would have been able to teach myself some first aid. Not that it helps you much now, or me. But maybe I could have done something."

The girl looked around, and Mayhem saw the exact moment when she noticed the lip of the open window. She glanced down at him, then back to the window, and he could have sworn he saw the slimmest trace of a smile. It was a look that sparkled not with hope, but with defiance.

"At least I'll know it isn't impossible to get out of this place. If you can make it, crow, any of us can, too."

She moved towards the wall with the wardrobe and the window, not looking at the large birdcage as she passed it, the cage she would be trapped inside shortly, if she didn't leave quickly.

The girl lifted her hands as high as she was able, her frail muscles straining as she stretched towards the open sill. When he was sure he wouldn't fall, Mayhem jumped from her hand to the wood, leaving red, sore marks on her hands, but relief coursed through his bones as he felt the wind wrap around him.

It didn't matter that he could no longer fly, at least not for now. It was enough knowing that he could stay out of Harrow's reach until he healed.

They both heard shuffling outside in the hallway, and it was enough to make the girl panic again. She looked for something sturdy, a stool or a box to stand on. The window was large enough for her to fit, and Mayhem thought that it might be possible for her to survive the fall from the roof if she landed right. He opened his mouth to let out a sound that closely resembled a wail, hoping that she would hurry.

Blue-eyes dragged the golden cage towards the window. Although it made the crow shudder, he knew it was her best hope. She pushed against it, only falling once or twice before she crushed it against the wall. The girl climbed atop it and reached for the windowsill, grabbing on tightly with the tips of her fingers. Mayhem watched as her nails dug deep and the girl pushed off the cage, causing it to wobble and hit the wall with steady thuds.

Harrow must have heard that.

He wished he could help her, drag her body up and through the window, but it was no use. She was too weak to get herself up on her own. After a disappointing fall, she jumped up several more times, barely able to hang on for more than a few seconds before giving up and slipping off. With no good grip on the cage, her feet gave way, and she crashed to the floor on her bottom, knocking the wind from her chest.

The girl looked up at Mayhem, her determination gone. She tried one last glance around the room for something larger, but there wasn't anything she'd have been able to move on her own. There was no escape for her.

"I'll see you on the other side."

Her voice was sad and lacked any confidence as it died off, the silence around them deafening. Blue-eyes gave a final half wave to the crow before she turned around and ran towards the door. She grabbed the knob and twisted it slowly. The door's hinges creaked again loudly and without care, as it cracked open. Mayhem wished, just once, that it was possible for her to find the front door and run. He wanted her to feel the grass beneath her feet again, to know how the sunshine felt against her skin.

Mayhem let himself *hope* for her.

And then the girl was gone, slipping between the door and sealing it closed again, leaving him as he was before he stepped foot into Harrow's room. Mayhem turned, determined to put his ordeal behind him, but first he had to forget the girl.

It was much easier when he didn't really care about the children in the house.

It was easier when he didn't know them.

Of course, it would have been less difficult if he couldn't feel the pain of his snapped wings pounding in his eardrums. Mayhem was never going to be afforded that luxury of forgetting. He dropped into a crouch on top of the wooden sill, black feathers rustling in the forgiving wind.

The crow closed his eyes, protected again by the height. He could escape when Harrow returned, after his wings had healed. Before that happened, he waited for the inevitable.

It took only moments.

His heart seized as if a dagger had been thrust through his chest at the sound of the young girl's scream.

Against guilt, height would be no protection after all.

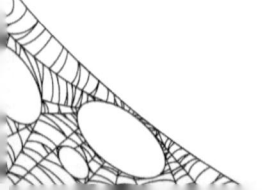

Chapter 8
The Rat

FLEA HAD BEEN WANDERING THROUGH THE TWISTING, UNENDING corridors for what felt like an eternity. He couldn't tell if he was retracing his steps or if the maze itself was shifting around him, its warped design teasing and mocking his every turn. Each room was a distorted echo of the last, yet subtly, horrifyingly altered—walls leaning at odd angles, shadows deepening in corners that seemed to breathe, and always, the same maddening silence, empty of any human trace.

He had hoped to find the others, to stumble upon the children or Blue again, but the labyrinth sprawled on, swallowing his every footstep and leaving him to worry, alone in the decaying halls. Flea trudged onward, the air thick and stale, clinging to his lungs. The floorboards beneath him creaked, but the noise didn't sound right—instead, it was like something whispering in guttural tones; voices bleeding through the wood. Shadows swayed and stretched, clawing at the walls, bending into sinister shapes that seemed to follow him with each step.

"aaahhhhh!"

Flea jumped, his fur standing on end. The scream echoed, twisting around him, trailing off with a sickening, muffled whimper. He thought to run, to retreat to whatever miserable safety he had left behind, but an irresistible pull forced him forward. On shaking legs, he crept into the darkness, whiskers twitching with every slow, hesitant step.

He turned a corner and froze. There, in the flickering candlelight, stood Blue. Her back was to him, her stance eerily still. Flea's heart seized. This was the girl he had abandoned, the one he'd left behind in a fit of self-preservation, and now her ghostly presence was waiting for him, a silent accusation in the dark. She didn't turn, didn't speak, but her form seemed to shimmer, both haunting and condemning, like she was nothing more than a manifestation of his own guilt.

In front of her, the demon appeared from the shadows.

Harrow's hollow sockets burned with a sickly plum glow; her face stretched into a ravenous grin. Each flicker of her candlelit fingers cast warped obscurities that crawled along the walls.

Harrow's melted hands seized Blue with a sickening, oozing grip, claws of molten wax grazing her face as the demon surged forward in a frenzy, eyes wild and mouth distended, gleaming in the dim light.

Blue seemed unable to move—rooted to the ground in her fear or clutched immobile by the very floorboards. The Hag's twisted form quivered with anticipation, nostrils flaring as she inhaled Blue's terror, exhaling a rasping, guttural laugh that rattled through the maze. Each touch seemed to sink Blue deeper into the monster's shadow, her outline blurring as if she were dissolving into the very darkness.

Waxen claws raked across Blue's cheek, and her scream

fractured the silence, fighting against the crushing weight as she clawed at the creature's wrists, slick with her own blood.

The sight of red against Blue's skin stopped the Hag cold. Harrow's waxen features knotted, the monstrous frenzy fading as if pulled back into a dark recess within her. Her grip slackened, and the horror in her expression softened... to something almost regretful. Harrow shuddered, trembling, her demonic rage giving way to a broken, maternal yearning.

"Shh, darling," Harrow whispered, almost tenderly, fingers brushing away the blood with surprising care, though the streaks of crimson seemed to pain her. She held Blue with a disturbing gentleness, fingers cradling her face, gazing at her like her mind was unraveling, torn between the urge to comfort and the searing instinct to feed.

Her moment of hesitation evaporated as quickly as it had come. Harrow's hunger reignited, sharper than before, and she twisted her face into a grotesque grin as she seized Blue's arm with renewed vigor. Her fingers melted, fusing with Blue's skin, the wax of her body swallowing Blue's limb. Harrow let out a rattling growl, and the shadows around them thickened, closing in with each sickening pull.

Blue's legs kicked weakly as Harrow dragged her backward, inch by inch, down the dim hallway. The once-familiar girl was barely visible beneath the limbs and oozing digits of the demon. Flea moved to follow them, but the waxy floor had already flowed over his right front paw. He yanked it out and the *SNN—AA—PP* of wax echoed down the corridor.

Harrow's gaze flicked back up, and she finally saw Flea, her face smeared with blood and gore. Her mouth opened in a bloodstained glower, chunks of flesh still clinging to her teeth, and her eyes widened in surprise. Harrow extended a dripping hand toward the rat, her voice low and filled with cruel satisfaction.

"Don't go, little one," she whispered, licking the blood from her lips. "I'm not done eating."

Frantic, Flea tried to orient himself, but the ever-shifting walls offered no familiar details to guide him. The walls began to undulate like waves on a turbulent sea, their patterns swirling and morphing into faces that leered at him. The floor beneath his feet trembled, threatening to give way to the abyss below.

So, he ran in whatever direction he could.

Flea's paws pounded against the floorboards, heart racing as he sprinted through the corridors, darkness swallowing his every step. He could hear her behind him—Harrow's slow, uneven footsteps, the wet drag of her melted limbs scraping across the floor, voice slithering through the hallways.

"Where are you running to, little Flea?" Her voice, sticky sweet, echoed all around him, seeping through the walls and curling into his ears. "There's no way out."

Every turn brought him deeper into the endless maze, each doorway leading only to another corridor, darker and narrower than the last. Flea's breathing came in short, ragged gasps as he darted through another doorway, heart hammering, only to find himself in a room he could swear he'd been in before—the same cracked molding on the wall, the same empty chair casting a long, warped shadow across the floor.

His body felt sluggish, the walls pulling at him, their surfaces warping around him, claws stretching out to snag his fur. His limbs grew heavy, each step harder than the last.

"You'll make the perfect little desert."

Flea's legs finally gave out, and he crumpled to the floor, chest heaving, his vision hazy as he strained to listen for Harrow's footsteps.

Silence.

The echoing mockery of her voice vanished, leaving only his pounding heartbeat in the stifling quiet.

Flea forced himself to look up, expecting to see her monstrous form lurking in the shadows. But the hallway was empty. No glistening waxen handprints trailed along the walls. No sickly glow pulsed from hollow eyes. Only the same worn wallpaper, cracked and peeling, lined the corridor.

His throat was dry, his fur damp with sweat as he backed away, still half-expecting Harrow to leap from the shadows.

The walls that had seemed to claw at him moments before were now bare, absent of life, covered only in dust and decay; the oppressive dread that weighed him down, now thin, like smoke dissipating in the air.

Flea took a shaky breath and pushed forward, fear ebbing into a wary trepidation, grabbing the floor with all fours, claws deep in the wood.

He staggered forward, erratic and lost, until he was truly alone, with nothing but the echoing screams in the distance from the girl he couldn't save, and the haunting cackles of the hag who taunted him.

Chapter 9
The Crow

His wings still ached terribly, even more now that the adrenaline was starting to wane. Mayhem didn't want to try to move them; the mere thought of it made him cry out in anguish.

The pain was the worst he had ever endured. A bird without wings was a travesty. It reminded Mayhem of something he heard once before, from children's voices reaching him through the walls.

"What do you call a fly without wings?"

A Walk, he remembered. That was exactly what he was now, a Walk. He could not understand what could have been so funny about it, but the children tittered anyway, hushed laughter as they sprinted through Harrow's house on the hill.

Still, he knew he must try. He worried the bones were more than broken, worried that Harrow had done more than just make him crumble beneath her fingertips. Her magic was something else, and while she never used it directly against him, he knew that he had severely underestimated her ruthlessness.

It had almost cost him his life.

The crow hesitated, but finally twitched them gently, one after the other, awaiting the damage.

Agony tore through his body like a thousand fiery needles piercing his skin and burrowing deep into his bones. He clenched his beak and squeezed his eyes shut, trying to contain the overwhelming pain that vibrated his core. Mayhem felt every nerve ending firing alive with electricity, sending shockwaves through his muscles and bones. As though he was on fire. A guttural caw escaped him as he tried to endure the torture.

Mayhem clenched his beak and closed his eyes tightly, trying to contain the urge to continue squawking. His wings, usually spread out, were now tightly folded against his back again, in a desperate attempt to shield himself. Even against his sides in their resting position, it felt like the hurt would ache for days and weeks to come. At least they could move and were not entirely useless; he might be able to fly again at some point.

But not now.

Robbed. Flight, taken from him in a second.

The door blew open by itself, strained to appease Harrow as she strode in with confidence. The sound of the door slamming against the frame echoed through the room, causing Mayhem's eyes to snap open in shock and surprise at the sudden disruption. Her sockets turned towards the corner Mayhem had been trapped in before the child had saved him, Harrow's brows pinching together, the sockets becoming distrustful slits when she recognized his absence.

"MAYHEM!" she screeched.

He didn't respond. His body curled tighter in on itself, on top of the sill. Though the crow could not quell the quake in his body, he would not stand down. Harrow searched frantically on the ground below for her once-trapped conquest, her hands curled into flaming fists. Her head swiveled to survey the caked floors and shadowed corners.

Mayhem awaited her soulless gaze with a steely determination, a rebellion he would never have dared before. And when her hollowed sockets turned to face him, the crow did not back down.

Harrow seemed surprised, the skin above her sockets pulling up into an unrecognizable expression as she looked back from the corner in which the crow had been trapped, certain to die, back to his place in her window.

Slowly, her lips curled into a small, deadly smile. The corners of her mouth lifted ever so slightly, like a predator preparing to pounce. Every movement of hers was calculated and precise, as if she held all the power in the world within her simple expression.

"How'd you get up there, my old friend, as battered up as you are?"

Mayhem cocked his head, wishing at this moment that he could jump from the window and leave the house on the hill.

"Surely it wasn't you on your own...my wax, perhaps? Could it be my magic softening to you? Have you gotten under my skin, bird, after all these years?"

Harrow glided across the floor, halting beneath the window. Mayhem shimmied back on the ledge, staying out of her reach, but not without a prickle of pain running like electricity through his plumage.

"Don't get your feathers in a knot, Mayhem, dear," she murmured, reaching out with flame fingers to caress the wood that outlined the window. "I have something else to play with for now."

Mayhem's gaze flickered reluctantly to the girl Harrow had dragged back with her, the one she now discarded like a broken doll. She lay slumped against the far wall, barely more than a shadow, her body frail and battered, a mess of darkened bruises and a raw, red wound on her shoulder. Even from across the room, he could see the lifelessness in her eyes, once bright but now dulled with agony and fading resolve.

Blue-eyes.

Guilt twisted in his chest, sharp and unforgiving.

Harrow caught the shift in his gaze, toward the girl slumped against the wall. With a slow, knowing smile, she turned, stepping deliberately between them, her dark form blocking his view. She tilted her head, watching him with a glint of mockery in her eye sockets. As if to emphasize her point, Harrow reached back with one flame-tipped hand, tracing it over the girl's broken form, shielding her entirely from his sight. Despite the relief he felt, free from her sightless gaze, Mayhem nevertheless felt discarded, as if he had disappointed her in some way.

Her attention now turned entirely onto the child, who quivered in the corner.

The blue-eyed girl was as broken as he was, mauled beyond repair. She was a bleeding mess, ichor settling underneath her; a gnarly wound from her shoulder where a fractured bone stuck out pulsed blood. She wept openly, her bottom lip quivering in anguish, as she pressed a hand to her missing flesh, her knees pulled close to her chest, wrapping her remaining arm around herself.

Even as the girl tried to make herself small and invisible, Mayhem knew it would make her more attractive to Harrow.

Who doesn't like to pounce on prey?

Harrow's fingers wrapped around Blue-eye's elbow, nearly crushing her bones as she pulled the girl up to her feet. The crow felt it almost wrench out of its socket, as if it was his wing, but somehow the girl managed to stay standing.

No amount of resistance would have kept her safe from Harrow's deadly games. Harrow picked the girl up with practically no effort at all, swinging her around until she faced the gilded bird cage.

"See, pretty bird? Aren't you happy this isn't you?"

Harrow's laughter echoed through the room as she gently closed the ornate cage, Blue-eyes trapped within. Red streaks of the girl's blood marred the bars as she tried to find her footing, tarnishing the shine. Harrow looked at her waxen hands, wiping the girl's gore from them in disgust.

Now that she was trapped beyond the bars of the cage, there was nothing she could do to escape it.

"I deplore silence, don't you?"

Mayhem assumed the wax demon was talking to him. He cocked his head in her direction and looked at her indifferently. Refusing to speak was his own act of defiance. It was the only thing he could give back to the blue-eyed girl for her sacrifice.

Disobedience.

"Petulant bird," Harrow chastised, "I don't know what's gotten into you. This is the game we play. Do not play the victim when you are the antagonist."

Mayhem knew he was no better than she was. The Hag was many things, but she was not a liar. Harrow was content living with her lot and expected those around her to do the same.

If only she didn't *enjoy it* as much as she did. It was in the malicious gleam freckled across her expression when her victims bled, and the unsettling laugh that escaped her throat when their entrails spilled across the floor.

"I am not crueler than those parents abusing their children and abandoning them. People in town are as monstrous as I am, they only wear better disguises. I cannot be blamed for *being*, Mayhem."

Her actions were despicable, and Mayhem loathed that the village they neighbored was equally wretched. The town sprawled, desolate and impoverished, its narrow streets lined with ramshackle buildings and rough, uncaring people. Greed and selfishness were their only motivations. They didn't hesitate to push their own children down the steep trail that wound along the hill where Harrow's house was nestled. One less mouth to feed was seen as a blessing across these lands, a sad reflection of the harsh realities of this place.

Blue-eyes set her jaw in a tight scowl.

"They do not *kill* people. Not like *you*."

Harrow and Mayhem's heads snapped in her direction, his eyes and Harrow's sockets locking onto her. Blue's eyes grew wide with the realization that she had spoken aloud, mouth slacking open in surprise at the sound of her own voice echoing through the empty room. The girl clamped her lips shut, a flush of new fear spreading across her cheeks.

"You beautiful girl," Harrow whispered softly. Her voice was like honey, sticky and sweet. "I wish you could see what we see. I wish you knew that they were not the people you thought they were. They are *exactly* like me, girl."

Mayhem always hated this part, the realization that they were sent like pigs for the slaughter.

He wanted to turn his head, unwilling to face the girl as slow understanding crawled over her features, but her jaw set. She did not cry, as he expected, did not shake. Her lips did not tremble. Her chest rose, as if with new air inside her lungs, her back straightening.

The small flames that flickered at the ends of each of the Hag's fingertips burned brighter, dancing in annoyance. She was used to this sort of unruliness from Mayhem, but never a child.

Harrow fed off their sorrow. She licked her lips from their distress. As much as she loved them, she needed them to survive; and Harrow never loved them as much as she loved herself.

"Foolish girl," she sneered, her saccharine-sweet voice replaced by her more familiar rasp that sent shivers down Mayhem's spine. Her words dripped malice and deception, the facade of love and affection masking her true intentions fled. "You're not so tough without your fingers, are you?"

Harrow reached her hand through the birdcage, which warped at her will, and wrapped her still flaming fingers around the girl's wrist. Blue tried to pull her arm back, but it was useless—Harrow's grip on her shattered shoulder kept her firmly in place. The damage was still fresh, skin and muscle barely knit together, and blood welled quickly, cascading down her arm as the wound was forced wider.

The crow could see her fingers twitch, helpless against the pain. The dark, gleaming trails of blood snaked over her hand. Harrow's eyes followed each drop with a chilling hunger. Almost reverently, she brought the girl's trembling hand to her mouth, running her tongue along her bloodied fingers, savoring the taste with dark, predatory satisfaction.

Mayhem couldn't look away.

The small girl struggled with all her might, but Harrow's flames held her fast, licking and devouring her hands with merciless heat. Blue-eyes pulled, desperate to free herself, yet the only reward was the smell of her burning flesh. Skin charred, darkening from brown to black. Her fingers twisted, the flesh stretching tight before splitting apart, revealing bubbling fat beneath, which sizzled and burst in viscous droplets. Fingernails, scorched and weakened, began to pop from their beds, tiny white flakes against the blackened skin, each crack and snap cutting through the air.

Blue-eyes could no longer scream. Her mouth hung open, but the only sound was the frantic, shallow gasps of air she managed between waves of agony. Her breaths came faster, caught somewhere between shock and terror, chest heaving as she tried and failed to fill her lungs, her voice lost beneath the crackling fire, swallowed up by the merciless heat that continued to consume her.

Muscle and tendon unraveled under the flames, melting away into liquid fat that dripped and sizzled onto the floor. Her bones strained against the heat, each tiny joint popping and cracking as the fire tore through her hands.

Mayhem screeched in terror, snapping Harrow out of her trance-like state with the deafening sound that echoed from him. The flames ceased to exist, disappearing into thin air like they were only a figment of the imagination.

"You're worse than me, you know, bird. Don't pretend to feel sorry for them. If you truly wanted to help them, you would. Instead, you're going to have to watch. Every last piece of this girl is on your broken wings, Mayhem. Every single child is going to die. Because. Of. You."

Still holding onto what was left of Blue's wrist, Harrow

pulled her hand up to her mouth and slipped what was left of the girl's index finger in between her lips.

The sharp sound of teeth meeting bone echoed in the dimly lit room. Harrow's jaw worked furiously as she gnawed her way down the girl's fingers, leaving behind bloody stubs, ruined flesh and severed tendons. There was a moment of nothing but the crunching and slurping sounds that came from the place where the two of them bonded together.

Mayhem was sure that the other children heard it wherever they were; a cacophony of screams and sobs and chomping. They would shiver, and cry for Blue-eyes, mourn her, just like they had with everyone else that had been victims of Harrow's games, in her lair. In her den.

In her house on the hill.

Part Two

"Pale warriors, death-pale were they all;
    They cried—'La Belle Dame sans Merci
    Thee hath in thrall!'"

-La Belle Dame sans Merci: A Ballad, John Keats

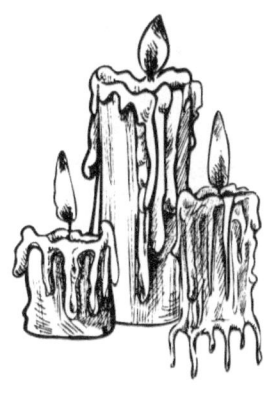

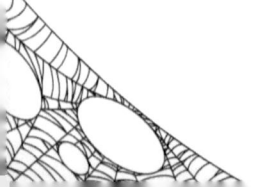

Chapter 10
The Crow

It didn't end with just Blue-eye's fingers.

"Will you walk into my parlor?"

The wax woman's voice, smooth and velvety like melted chocolate, filled the room, as the girl stared back with a tear-streaked face. It felt to Mayhem as though the girl's very soul was being pulled out through her eyes, leaving behind nothing but an empty shell. They were like oceans, reflecting the pain and confusion inside her; her expression blank, as if she had retreated into herself to escape the harsh reality of her cage.

The room felt heavy with emotion, the air thick and stifling. Harrow's rhyme echoed off the walls, haunting and sorrowful, spiders and their webs, flies and their curiosities.

As Harrow continued, reciting with perfect precision a poem that Mayhem recognized immediately, he narrowed his eyes and watched with subdued interest. Harrow was at least predictable in this, and the crow felt his panic subside from the routine alone. He knew what came next, just like the others before this girl. Harrow's unexpected capture of him was only a small infraction. Whilst his wings ached, a permanent reminder of the damage she could do, he would make sure his mistake would never be repeated.

Mayhem turned his eyes back to the girl, keeping Harrow's pacing in his peripherals. Blue-eyes sat in a pool of dark red blood, the jagged wound of her hand steadily leaking, despite the makeshift bandage she had torn from her shirt.

The tension in the room was as thick as cream, richer than the bowl left out for Old Tomas's cat in the village, who was too lazy to chase him off when the crow came around to drink from it in the evenings. Everything in the room seemed to ache with the girl's pain, vibrating in sync with her heartbeat, and the ground beneath Harrow's feet rippled.

The house felt hungry, drinking in the girl's blood, feeding off her fear as if it had been starved of it.

Purring.

"Mayhem, she's quieter than the rest of them, don't you think?" Harrow turned to him and worried her lip. "After all, I've done for them, I get nothing in return. All I've ever wanted was to love them. For them to love me. Everyone I love leaves me, bird."

Harrow took a cautious step closer to the blue-eyed girl along the windowsill. She instinctively recoiled further into the confines of her small cage. The metallic bars cast long shadows across her face, highlighting her wide blue eyes and trembling lip, bitten by rose tinged teeth. She clutched at the thin fabric of her tattered shirt, as if it were her only source of comfort.

It was no use. Harrow's fingers trembled as she gripped the bars, willing them to yield. The metal groaned in protest, softening like warm clay, and slowly, she bent the bars apart. Wax from her fingertips dripped onto the warped gold, hissing as the bars twisted open.

The last barrier between her and the child was gone.

Blue-eyes couldn't know how horrid her death was going to be, but Mayhem could see flashes of acceptance cross her features as Harrow's wrinkled hands pulled the girl up from her fetal position and into her cold embrace.

"I loved you when no one else would, girl. You should thank me."

The woman's grip tightened around the girl, lifting her off the ground with ease. As she opened her mouth in a menacing grin, Mayhem caught a glimpse of the rows and rows of sharp, pointed teeth glimmering in the faint light. He shivered, the tremor aggravating his broken wings, his heart pounding against his chest. Saliva stretched across Harrow's incisors as she widened her mouth, lowering it to the girl's ear as if she was sharing an important secret.

Instead of the world's softest whisper, Mayhem heard the gnashing of Harrow's lips as they smacked together. The girl's skin tore and ripped like wet paper, exposing raw muscle and sinew. Harrow pulled greedily at the girl's earlobe until it detached from her head, dangling limply, tiny in her bloody jaws, mouth puckering as if waiting for a kiss until the lobe was sucked past her lips. She swallowed greedily, like an oyster from its shell. The gruesome display of violence and power was almost sensual for Harrow, making it even more painful to watch.

The girl that saved Mayhem lost so much blood; the light dimmed behind her eyes. Her head lolled to the side, presenting Harrow more flesh, as the hag latched onto the open shoulder wound, greedily sucking the remaining life force from her victim.

The crow yearned for Blue-eyes to turn her gaze

towards him, even though he knew he was responsible for her fate. Instead, all he could see was the back of Harrow's head, the fresh cracks in her neck forming as she twisted and turned, steaming hot wax running down her back as she entered her feeding frenzy. And when the girl fell limp at last, when Mayhem was sure that she was gone, the wax woman wrapped her arms around her and hugged her tightly.

The crow twitched his aching wings, a heavy reminder that her death was his burden to bear, etched deep into his bones. Each beat of his wings ached, a raw pulse of guilt. He watched, unwillingly entranced, as Harrow absorbed what remained of Blue-eyes. It was a ritual both reverent and consuming, her obsessive love swallowing her whole, as if this final act could immortalize the girl he couldn't save.

Piece by delicate piece, Harrow took her in.

The slope of the girl's collarbone lay exposed, the skin thin and translucent, split and bruised, bone shining through like cracked porcelain, framed by threads of drying blood. Her cheek, freckled and tender, was streaked with blood spatter, the golden flecks now darkened, clinging to her skin like stars drowned in shadow. Her lip, once soft and pink, now hung open, a pale shade of white, with teeth marks where she had bitten down, hard, the line of red mingling with the faint remnants of her final scream.

Blue-eye's elbow, delicate in its smallness, bent unnaturally, bone poking through the skin, marred by smeared, streaking sinew. Her calf, a graceful line, was torn and punctured, veins visible in their twisted patterns beneath the ravaged skin, the faint curve suggesting a future that would never come. And her ankle—bare, bloodied, yet still oddly intact—had a slenderness that seemed almost surreal against the grime.

In each fragile piece, there lingered a soft beauty that, in life, would have filled the air around her with life. With every tender morsel, Harrow tasted more than flesh—she tasted the promise of what might have been, the raw potential of a girl just beginning to bloom.

Harrow devoured her, each bite an act of bitter reverence.

And when she finally stepped to the side, wiping her mouth with a long, slender hand, the girl was gone.

It was as if she never existed at all.

"Another ear for me to hear..."

Mayhem turned his head away as blood pooled on the carpet. Harrow felt no need to clean up the mess she made. Scraps of flesh and gore spread out before her, and despite how gruesome the scene looked, Mayhem was almost grateful. It was typical of Harrow to play with her meals before they died—cat-like. This almost seemed like mercy. Almost...*gentle.*

"Crows collect shiny things, right Mayhem?" Harrow spoke to him as she glided through her room, removing a severed ear from her teeth, flipping it through her fingers like a coin. She caressed it, thumb rubbing over the thin cartilage, like a token to spend or a medal she had won.

Trying as he might to keep his eyes turned away from her, Mayhem was drawn to her sated purr, like a moth to a flame. He watched as she floated to the drawer of her dresser, opening the creaking wood, and dropped the girl's ear deep into its depths.

"You see what I collect, of course. You're the only one that has. It's an art, you know, the magic I wield here. Truthfully, bird, I don't think I'll ever know the full extent of my capabilities within this house. This is all party tricks, really."

She would reclaim it later, would string the ear up into one of the corners of her moving halls and wait for the children to sneak through them. Mayhem didn't know if they noticed the severed appendages, they were hidden by darkness and layered in old webs, but Harrow would always know where they were. She used them against one another. The severed tools were not a trophy, but another tool for her to catch the children.

"She was different from the rest of them, I think. She was brave. Good, that she's gone. Their hopelessness tastes more delicious."

Harrow closed the drawer and tapped her lips with the wicks that topped each finger. The flames returned, caressing her mouth hungrily, blood droplets around her lips sizzling into the air, fresh melted wax smoothing over whatever had been left of the girl after Harrow had gorged, until even that was gone. She preened herself with fire.

"Was it her that protected you?"

There was no one else, Harrow was aware of that. She was not asking Mayhem for an answer; she was taunting him. Making him mourn the girl that saved him from her grip.

"Talk to me, bird. Tell me how much it hurts."

Harrow walked to the windowsill, where Mayhem flinched. His weakness was apparent, but the crow was past the point of caring. She made no move to grab him, she only looked at him, her head tilted to the side, then blinked, her lids closing for a second over the empty cobwebbed voids.

"What is it, Mayhem? Don't tell me you *care* for them." Her laugh echoed within the room. It filled his head. Her fleshy breath tickled his feathers like an apology.

She was horrid, terrible, and cruel. Harrow would haunt

the crow until his dying breath. Even if he wanted to, caring for the children was not an option. It only brought pain. Mayhem opened his beak, sighing his trauma until the last vestige of air had escaped his lungs, his silent cry a tribute to the girl and her silence, her bravery, her death.

Harrow looked at him expectantly, and the victorious gleam in her eye sockets echoed the defeat that was mirrored in his.

"I cannot, Harrow." He finally whispered in return.

Chapter 11
The Rat

FLEA'S LUNGS FELT ON FIRE, HIS BREATH RAGGED AND PAINFUL AS he turned the corner and, all at once, found the children. He had been running for hours, covering as much of the maze as he could, frantically trying to find an escape, even knowing it wouldn't happen.

They cowered in a large room, sinking into the corners, crouching, folding into themselves in an attempt to disappear. As if it would make a difference, should Harrow find them. They had nothing to worry about, though, not after the wax woman took Blue. She would be satiated for a few days more with her fill, chewing on snapped bones and crawling back into the hole she lived in.

Making sure they wouldn't see him, the rat crouched back into the wall and moved along it, leaving their tear-stained faces and heaving sobs behind him as he hid. Blue's death was as much their fault as it was his. It would take Flea a few days to get over it, the rage and guilt he felt for them and for himself.

Inside the walls always felt safest for him, as Flea could

hear what was happening on either side. Unfortunately, however, the rat never quite knew where he was, though that wasn't a new concept during his travels within the maze.

When he couldn't breathe, hyper-aware of how close the walls were on each side, Flea looked for a quick exit. With the maze decaying throughout time, it crumbled. Holes were scattered throughout the baseboards and lower walls, chewed through by the other critters he always felt but never saw—ones that came before him.

Harrow kept them all away from each other, isolating Flea from any ounce of hope.

Sooner, rather than later, he squeezed through a particularly small opening.

Emerging into the dim light of a dusty room, Flea scurried across the cracked floorboards, his heart pounding in his chest. The air was heavy with an ancient mustiness, and cobwebs hung like gossamer drapes from the corners of the room. As he paused to catch his breath, a faint disorientation made him pause.

He always felt lost here, but this room seemed particularly new. It reminded him of a foyer.

And before him, just outside of the opening, was a door.

Flea hesitated, his whiskers twitching as he contemplated the door in front of him. It stood tall and imposing, its wood dark and weathered with age. Its glass knob gleamed dully in the faint light filtering through the grimy windows, beckoning to him like a promise against the oppressive darkness of the house.

Flea approached the door cautiously, his paws making barely a whisper against the dusty floor. The silence in the room pressed in on him, intensifying his sense of foreboding. He felt like an intruder coming across a long-forgotten secret, and for a moment, Flea hesitated, his heart hammering. He never ventured this far, and the thought of what lay on the other side of the door filled him with both fear and excitement.

It could be the door Blue had talked about, though, of course, this one had a knob. Hadn't the girl said the door she saw was knob-less?

Flea flung himself at the door, panic flooding every movement. It charged his bones, fueled his desperation, the need to escape ready to burst out of his body.

He needed to be free.

All thoughts of the children left him—all that mattered was the taste of the clean air that would infiltrate his lungs, a life free of the maze.

Rationalizing excuses echoed through his skull, clinging to every last selfish act he'd ever committed. He wouldn't have time to go back and tell the children. They wouldn't believe him anyway, even if he did, treating him just like they had Blue, as if he was crazy, and then no one would be able to leave.

Flea bit into the door, his sharp teeth sinking into the rotted wood. It splintered slightly under the pressure, a painful jolt shooting through his jaw. He pulled, testing if he could tear a way through, but the fibers held firm.

He clamped down again, chewing at the splinters, trying to work his way through, but it was futile. Flea's teeth scraped and ached, the wood refusing to yield fast enough.

Desperation gnawed at him as much as he gnawed at the door.

Frustrated, Flea fastened his jowls and steadied himself for another pull, using every muscle he possessed to lock in and tear the door from his hinges. He yanked, hard. Again. And again.

By the fifteenth or sixteenth time, he could have collapsed from exhaustion. His body trembled, and he panted, furious with himself. Rearing up onto both feeble legs, using what was left of the strength nestled in his fore-arms, the rat scratched his claws against the glass-knobbed door. His strength waned, draining with each worthless attempt.

The door taunted him, solemn and sturdy, refusing even to shift an inch, despite whatever energy he put into his teeth and claws.

Realization hit Flea like a punch to the gut. This was a far crueler, more torturous fate than not knowing about the door at all. He stood mere feet from freedom, robbed of his escape. There would be no soft velvet-like grass beneath his paws, no safety of a burrow to hide him from the sun, only this maze, these hallways full of grime, for the rest of his life.

The rat's hatred for Blue burned like a fire. She had given him hope, only to crush it and leave him feeling even more alone than before. Flea knew, deep down, that he would always be alone in this desolate place, with no one but himself for company.

It enraged him, horrified him.

Splinters dug into the pads of his feet, the raw open sores making him wince as he finally dropped onto all fours. If Blue was dead, it would be easier knowing that no false hope would befall him ever again.

Flea retreated, trying not to look back at the door that led to the outside world. Instead, he curled up against the wall nearest the hole he'd come out of, wrapping his flesh around his cold, tired feet and digging his snout into his own fur.

For now, with nowhere else to go and no one left to save, the rat slept.

Chapter 12
The Crow

MAYHEM COULDN'T FLY. IT WAS A TRAVESTY; HE HAD NEVER realized how much he depended on his wings, or how desperately he needed to get away from Harrow, even only for a little while. His feathers bristled, knowing it would be impossible to jump from his sill and go to the village—that was what had come so naturally all of his life. The very act of moving was denied to him. Even if he always came back, the break from the atrocities that happened here was a necessity.

The stench of discarded flesh emulated from the room, wafting up to him, funneled by the air's current through its only open window. The tang of coppery blood made his body rebel, shaking in hunger.

He fought his own body's desires to devour.

The deeply rich, satisfying thickness of blood made his tongue salivate. Had it been a small animal, he would have had no hesitation. His natural hunger would have driven him to attempt to steal a portion. A chunk.

Yet this had been the girl that saved him.

Mayhem lowered his head, feathers rippling in a frustrated quiver. The broken bones would take weeks to mend on their own—if they ever did. At least now, he could flex his wings without the searing agony that once paralyzed him. It felt like progress, however slight. For a fleeting moment, the dull, throbbing ache faded, granting him a fragile illusion of relief. But Mayhem wasn't fooled. The numbness wasn't comfort—it was a harbinger. His body felt leaden, weighed down by exhaustion, each moment sinking him deeper into its grip. The cold gnawed at his very marrow, more biting than before, and no matter how fiercely he willed it, the relentless tremors coursing through him refused to cease.

The reality of his situation sunk into his belly like a heavy stone. His body was shutting down.

Mayhem turned away from Harrow's room, no longer able to stomach the sight. The wax woman was pacing endlessly, her movements eerily fluid yet unnervingly mechanical, her dripping feet squelching against the slick remains littering the floor. Chunks of flesh and bone, remnants of the girl she had consumed hours ago, lay scattered like discarded refuse, a macabre mosaic smeared across the room. Each step the creature took sent a fresh ripple through her melting form.

The stench wafted out, rich and heady, hitting Mayhem like a blow to the gut. He clenched his beak shut, his feathers ruffling involuntarily as he fought the wave of hunger gnawing at him.

Damn it, that *smell*. It was so maddeningly good. His stomach twisted, both in horror and from an unbearable craving that he couldn't suppress. It clung to him, a primal ache clawing its way through his mind with a single, insistent truth: *That's food.*

And yet, she was ruining it. That shambling, dripping

thing, crushing perfectly good meat into the floor, trampling all that life-rich juice into the muck. Wasteful. It was all such a stupid, infuriating waste. His talons twitched, his throat tightening as the scent pulled him in, despite the bile rising alongside it. But no. *No.* That had been a girl.

Mayhem staggered back a step, wings trembling at his sides, a deep growl building in his chest. The conflict seared through him, shame and hunger battling like warring storms.

He felt his insides churn, bile hot and bitter against the back of his throat—not because of the carnage, but because of himself. He wanted to tear into those pieces, taste the marrow, the fat, to fill the gnawing emptiness inside of him, a loathing so sharp it made his feathers bristle, but it wasn't enough to extinguish the hunger.

His nature screamed at him, loud and insistent, clawing at every thread of reason he clung to. Mayhem shut his eyes tightly, as if the darkness might silence the craving. But it didn't. Instead, it made it worse, the scent and image of the discarded meat all the more vivid, like it had been burned into his mind.

He tried to think of anything else.

Mayhem turned his attention to the rotted exterior of the home. It had once been beautiful, sleek. Now the wood jutted up at odd angles. The ceiling was close to near deterioration. The once pointed iron rods that decorated the rooftops had dulled to a thunderstorm black and were eroded from the weather.

Harrow sucked the life out of everything around her.

Unlike the ever-fluctuating, fluid nature of the house, the surrounding area remained constant. The dirt trails that led up to the Victorian estate sat empty, the rolling hills degraded from the cold that crawled over their quaint land.

From this height, the village nestled like dull iron, gray and squat, no hint of life or redemption about it. As dead as the eyes of all its damned inhabitants, and of the girl he kept trying not to think about.

Mayhem waited until the woman of wax turned away, then shimmied himself over until his chest was flush with the edge of the window frame. The fall was immense. What had been nothing to him hours before, now an un-surviv-able barrier without the aid of the wind cushioning his descent. He was meat. Hitting the ground from up here would be the same as the effect of the butcher's hammer in the village on the meat he tenderized.

What an awful word. Exactly like Harrow. Brutalizing meat and calling it love.

"Surely you're not that dumb, bird."

Mayhem didn't give her the satisfaction of turning to face her, though he couldn't say that it was his infinite confidence that prevented it. Moreover, he didn't want Harrow to be able to talk him out of it; it would be too easy.

"If you attempt to leave that sill in that condition, Mayhem, you'll die. What a silly way to die, don't you think? I'd rather not find my oldest friend splattered across gravel."

Mayhem looked down and shook out his tail feathers. It would be so easy, just the slip of a claw, a foot misplaced, and he would go tumbling down. His eyes caught the piece of wood that protruded from the roof again. It was only ten feet below him at most, but the wood was thin. He didn't know how much weight it could hold. It might crumble the second it bore his small frame. Though he wasn't heavy, it looked fragile.

"What a waste." Harrow hissed, and the crow could envision the rows of teeth that lined her mouth as she snarled at him. The pull of the golden cage, empty again—waiting for him to return to it, seemed to ruffle his wing. Almost like suction, his weight shifting slightly before he corrected himself. Though there were guests that frequented it, there was no doubt she had made it for him, and him alone.

This was possibly his last chance to be free of it.

Mayhem's beak snapped shut.

He stepped off the windowsill.

The sudden rush of wind smoothed the feathers on his chest as he slid the short distance on the rough stone roof tiles, and then he was over the edge. Mayhem hung suspended for a moment, the urge to open his wings so insistent, muscles screaming at him to do what came naturally. Bolts of agony lanced into his ribs, as his broken wings opened only a fraction before slamming back against his body in revulsion to the pain.

It was so much further than ten feet.

Mayhem's translucent eyelids flicked away the moisture clouding his vision as he tried to concentrate, pinpointing the exact moment he would collide with the wooden slab below. He bent his knees, bracing himself, but without his wings to slow his descent, he slammed into the plank chest first. The impact drove the air from his lungs in a single, brutal gasp. One wing tore free, yanked open by the sheer force of the collision. Feathers burst loose in a violent spray, drifting away in slow, elegant spirals toward the distant ground below, as his wide eyes remained frozen in stunned disbelief.

The wood bent as he gained his footing, bowing and bobbing, but it didn't break. Mayhem hadn't planned on surviving the fall, but now that he had, his overwhelming sense of survival sharpened his instincts. Away from the distraction of Harrow, and the succulent meat that he'd left behind, the crow could find his focus; the wind bent around him, caressing him as he fought to remain balanced without the help of his wings.

When the wood stopped bouncing and Mayhem felt himself steady, he peered over its edge. He was levels and levels above the ground. The short fall he had just taken felt like an eternity, and the next platform below him was at least three times the distance.

His last feat would be impossible to replicate, wings beginning to feel cold, body drained and breathless. Though Mayhem was stable with his claws dug several inches into the jutted piece of the rooftop, just looking down made him dizzy.

Instead of facing the drop, the crow looked from side to side, hoping to find another way out of the clutches of the house. Though the building was decorated with iron fili- gree and luxurious molding, he couldn't be sure of what state he would find each piece in. He had been lucky with his wooden slab; there was every reason to believe the next fixture would collapse from years of rot and neglect.

The only viable option remained a landing that was several yards over. It would not be easy to reach. Mayhem wouldn't be able to just step off his plank and fall onto it like the last attempt. The landing closely resembled a balcony, attached to a separate window he'd flown by several times over, making him think that it could have been made with more durable materials in its prime.

Though the wind was his friend, it could only aid him by amplifying his natural ability. It could not interfere with magic; they were two opposing forces, each restricted within the confines of their universal duties.

Before he could think twice, Mayhem unclenched his

claws and launched himself off the board that protruded from the rooftop. Instead of tucking his wings, he unfurled them, letting out a howl as the black feathers reached his full wingspan. The crow felt the wind between them, swirling around him as it helped carry him to the platform below.

For a moment, it felt like flying. He couldn't do much more than let his wings glide him towards his destination. The urge to use them to soar was hard to resist, if not for the scorching pain that flowed through his shattered bones, Mayhem might have tried.

When he was nearly there, a loud *crack* rent the air. Mayhem spun his head towards the window he had once lived on, and his eyes widened in terror as the slab of wood he just left came barreling towards him.

It was much faster than the crow in the state he was in, and small, sharp splinters and wedges from it bounced off the house, shrapnel sent along his flight path. Mayhem twisted himself to avoid the worst of it, but his back was suddenly hit by a much larger object.

His wings, once spread wide and graceful, curled in tight in a desperate attempt to regain control as his body spun wildly through the air. He collided beak first into the unforgiving window with a wet thud, feathers scattering in all directions, before he fell to the platform. The impact knocked him senseless, leaving him dazed and disoriented amidst broken pieces of the wood that had caught him.

Mayhem's head twitched on the landing, his body flattened against the roof panels, eyes fluttering open and shut.

Still alive, miraculously.

The crow felt the house moving underneath him, breathing, alive, expanding and contracting.

Mayhem didn't want to shut his eyes, wasn't sure what he would wake up to if he let go now, but he had no choice. The dark rose, and the light spiraled down, into a place where the pain no longer hurt, the wind no longer blew, and his chest no longer rose.

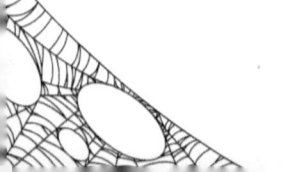

Chapter 13
The Rat

CRAASSSHHHH!

The cacophonous sound shook the ground beneath the rat's feet, the suddenness and intensity of it leaving him with little time to think or react.

Each eyelid flickered, one at a time, every blink bringing him back to a groggy state of awareness. Flea's body was tightly wound, tail curled against him and pressed against the floorboards, as if to anchor him to that very spot, but he defied gravity. His body moved before his brain could think, righting himself on all fours and desperately swinging his head to find the source of the sound.

His heart pounded as he came up empty.

The crash hadn't originated in the room he occupied.

Flea turned to haphazardly lick down hair that stood on end, flattening the fur on his back into a wet sticky mop, content knowing he wasn't in any immediate danger.

To no surprise, the door he'd found hours ago was gone. It was as if someone had plucked him from his sleep and placed him in an entirely different segment of the house.

Harrow's doing, most likely.

The rat turned away from where the door—and its false hope—used to stand. He looked for the largest opening available along the floorboards. It wasn't hard to find, the corner of the new room was rotted to its bones, leaving a sizable gap with long abandoned webs weaved across it.

Tempted forward by the need to identify the source of the loud crash, Flea squeezed through the hole and tumbled through the floorboards into the darkness below. The brittle wood had given way with a groan, snapping beneath his weight, sending him into a chaotic freefall.

Flea's tiny claws scrambled for purchase, catching nothing but splinters before he hit the ground with a thud. Pain shot through his side as he landed awkwardly on a pile of damp debris, ears ringing from the impact.

Moonlight filtered in from a crack above, casting a dim glow on the dank, uneven floor littered with broken wood and rusted metal scraps. Flea shook his body, trying to rid himself of the dirt and splinters clinging to his fur, though the ache in his left leg made him wince. He flexed it cautiously; it didn't feel broken, but the sharp sting made it clear he wasn't unscathed.

Looking up, he saw the jagged edges of the broken boards far above him—he must have fallen at least a story, though it didn't quite make sense if the glass-knobbed door he'd been in front of, hours before, was the one to freedom.

Flea's tail flicked nervously as he took in his surroundings, uneasy of the magic that he could never fully understand here. All that he knew was that the door to freedom was now too far out of reach, and he had little hope that he would come across it ever again. He and the maze would always be at odds with one another.

The walls rumbled around him in response.

With a curious twitch of his whiskers, Flea scurried

forward, following the path that never seemed to turn, though it was far too long to be the normal length of the house, disappearing into the darkness, flanked on either side by the familiar walls closing in on him.

After walking for only a few minutes, the rat's ears perked up as he finally caught the faint sound of whispering coming from the other side of the wall. He crept closer to listen. Flea was no longer desperate for the children that hid beyond the wall, no longer panicked in an attempt to reach them, but he was happy to know that they hadn't gone very far. He would always be able to find them, and that knowledge was a comfort he couldn't properly understand.

As Flea closed in, he noticed a faint light seeping through another crack in the wall. He rushed to the hole and pressed himself against the cold wood to look through the opening.

Children. The rat counted them. 1, 2, 3, 4...and that was it. No trace of the girl he'd abandoned, the one he had left to die.

They were all crowded around a window, looking at each other with fear and trepidation. One knocked on the window quietly with a knuckle, desperate to get the attention of whatever lay outside of it. Another wrinkled the hair above their eyes, furrowing in deep concentration.

Flea's sharp nails caught on a jagged sliver of wallpaper as he struggled to get a better look at them and listen. With a sudden jolt, he pulled back, causing the already peeling paper to rip with a loud and gut-wrenching pop. The sound echoed through the room.

Despite his best efforts to recover, Flea fell forward on the floor, somersaulting before the children. The sudden noise made them jump to their feet, their eyes wide with astonishment. Flea scrambled to his paws and tried to compose himself, but the damage was done.

For a moment there was silence as the children and Flea regarded one another. He could see the fear in their eyes, the uncertainty of what his unexpected appearance meant for them. The last time they had seen him was across the shoulders of Blue. Seeing him confirmed the death sentence for the child they all had so much faith in.

"Oh my god, look at you. You're so dirty! Where have you been? Where's Lucy?"

"Please don't tell me she's gone. Please don't, rat. *Please.*"

It was too late for all of them.

His gaze darted around the room, avoiding eye contact with any of them. The question had come from someone, but he couldn't bring himself to look and find out who had asked it. It had sounded like Smalls, her voice barely above a whisper, but he couldn't be too sure. Their muffled sobs fell to the floor, sinking softly past the floorboards.

Moonlight seeped into the room through the window behind them, its glass fractured with a spiderweb of cracks radiating from a single point of impact. Several fractures in the glass spread across the pane, letting in rainbows of light twinkling across the floor. Flea's gaze locked onto it, unable to pull away.

It looked as though something—or someone—had been trying to get *in.*

He stood frozen, breath shallow, his body tense, as seconds stretched into eternity, ignoring the stifled cries of the children mourning their lost friend.

But the silence held, and nothing moved.

Flea slowly crawled towards the window, the children following suit, as if suddenly remembering what it was that had captured their attention before his unexpected arrival. They reached high on their toes, hands grasping the lip of the wood intently.

Flea grabbed onto the pant leg of the closest child and worked his way up to the glass. He wasn't sure what he would see on the other side, but what he hadn't expected was a dead-looking crow, feathers in disarray and chest rising too slowly.

Bird.

Chapter 14
The Crow

He blinked in surprise at the sight before him——rolling green hills, dotted by wildflowers as far as the eye could see. And as a gentle breeze wrapped around him, carrying with it the pungent scent of earth, he couldn't help but feel like he had stumbled upon a magical world, far beyond what he knew, though the air of similarities were difficult to overlook.

Those hills were not unlike the ones that crouched just outside of his windowsill, within sight of the house on the hill. Spotted with living greenery, they were less desolate, delicate blades of grass swaying softly in the broad sunlight. The sun was another anomaly to its usual gloomy haze, and Mayhem squinted against its harsh light. It was a mirror; a happier, brighter, more colorful version of the world he knew.

His tail feathers quivered, the vibrations rattling through his small body until he had to shake out his feet from the anxious ticks. Mayhem winced, expecting the anguishing pain of his broken wings to accompany the movement, but none did.

The crow spread his wings out wide, stretching the tendons so much that they almost separated from muscle and bones. It felt like he hadn't done that in eternity, like he was denied the *freedom of his primal instincts, even if it had just been a few hours.*

Click.

Click.

Click.

The sound was small and almost inscrutable, but Mayhem could hear it clear as day. It seemed to call out to him. Its rhythm was steady and precise, like a dancer's footsteps or the gentle tapping of rain on a windowpane. Every beat felt like a secret message just for him, drawing him closer with each passing moment.

Click.

Click.

Click.

"You need to leave!"

As he stared out into the distance, lost in thought, distracted by the make-believe realm he'd been sent to, the high-pitched voice pierced through his daydreams. He spun around and was met with the sight of the small, blue-eyed girl. Her face was smudged with dried candle wax, and her eyes were filled with terror as she walked towards the crow perched on the landing. The bird flapped his wings and pressed himself against the old Victorian windowpane, his black feathers ruffled in fear.

"Do not be deceived, crow. This is what she wants! You must go, now!"

Bits of her face seemed to melt as she spoke, as if each word came with consequence. The sun seemed hotter, a blistering heat that she would never survive in her waxy state. Mayhem watched as streams of softened wax fell from her chin, a pool of it forming on the ground. Her sockets drooped; her features changed. The girl's mouth hung open, locking in place as she took several erratic steps towards him.

"Get out of here before she gets you, before it's too late..."

She was no longer the brave girl that saved him, the girl that tried to escape the house on the hill; she was something else. The girl was a product of Harrow, a victim...but also a monster.

She hurled herself at Mayhem, jumping from the ground to where he stood, with ease. He flapped his wings and jumped, hoping they could hold his weight. They felt sore from disuse, and no matter how hard he tried to fly, gravity kept him tethered to the ground. This place was not the dream he wished for, but a nightmare disguised.

As the dead girl moved towards him in a deep, predatory crawl, the clicks grew louder, echoing throughout his eardrums. The sound was everywhere, the girl was everywhere; Mayhem couldn't escape them both.

Mayhem would need to wake soon, and who knew what lay just beyond his closed eyes? He would have to face the children he had abandoned; he would have to face Harrow.

Click.

Click.

Click.

The young girl's mouth stretched open, revealing a frightening display of multiple rows of sharpened teeth. Her eyes glinted with a twisted eagerness as she reached out for her prey, ready to deliver him to her master at long last.

As his eyelids fluttered open, Mayhem was not met with the harsh glare of sunlight. There were no green hills or magical wind that wrapped around him.

Mayhem was a raw nerve, splayed open from the whetted scissors of his nightmare.

Click.

Click.

Click.

The bird pushed himself off the ground until he was upright, the sting of his broken wings cementing him back into reality. Everything was pain. His head, from the window. His body, from the fall. His wings curled limp at his sides.

Click.

Click.

Click.

Mayhem turned his head, wincing as his over-stretched tendons tightened. The window to the balcony was large and intimidating, lines webbing from his point of impact, but he knew that was where the terrible clicking came from. After his vision cleared, the crow's gaze honed in on a dark figure scurrying against the glass of the window.

More scratches against the pane, louder now. Mayhem could no longer ignore it, and he focused until he could just make out a large rat perched on its hind legs behind the glass. Its sharp claws were outstretched as it repeatedly batted at the point he had hit, determined to gain his attention. The crow watched in fascination; his beady eyes locked on the rodent.

Bird.

It wasn't a sound—at least, not in the way sounds were supposed to be, more like an idea, a flash in his mind. The word hit Mayhem like a slap. It wasn't a thought that had come from him. It was just... there. Sudden. Unsettling. He blinked, shaking his head as though trying to dislodge it, breaking eye contact.

Mayhem huffed, the weird sensation still lingering in

his skull. He turned his gaze back to the rat. And—*again.*
That sudden *flash.*

Bird.

This time, it was louder, clearer. As if the word had some kind of weight to it. He felt... unnerved. Mayhem glanced around again, as if the thought had come from the trees themselves. Nothing. Just the sway of leaves, the hum of insects.

The rat's gaze never wavered; his eyes focused on Mayhem like he was the only thing that mattered in the world.

And then—*the word again.* Louder now.

BIRD!

It was unmistakable. The creature had dropped onto all fours, his body poised as if he'd never moved; it lowered itself back down, coiling its long pink tail around its paws, small, black eyes fixed on him. Watching.

The rodent wasn't just watching him anymore—he was *doing* something. Speaking, somehow, without speaking.

"I hear you," Mayhem said, the words coming out in a daze. He wasn't sure if he meant to say it out loud or not. But the weight of that thought—of the rat's thoughts—was too strong to ignore.

The creature blinked at him again, his mouth opening slightly, like he was about to say something. It latched its teeth onto the nearest wood piece, seemingly out of frustration.

And then, with a twitch of his whiskers, the rat looked at him intently—**Me.**

Mayhem swallowed, his mind racing. The rat didn't move, but his eyes locked onto Mayhem's, waiting for him to understand.

Bang!

A large smack reverberated against the window. It hit just right, right where the glass was at its weakest. The circular rings of his previous collision snapped, sending shards of glass exploding in different directions. Mayhem jumped to avoid the shrapnel as it flew at him, threatening to slice through his soft skin.

The window lay shattered, a gaping hole in the center where a small fist had made an impact. Hazy moonlight streamed through the jagged edges, casting shadows on the floor. A young boy stood beside the rat, his eyes wide with shock and disbelief. He examined his hand, now covered in blood and scratches from the broken glass.

Peering from behind them both were a group of children, huddled against the cool paneled walls. The small figures trembled, their delicate hands covering their mouths to muffle the noises they were unable to hold back. Reverberating sounds echoed through the halls—Harrow would surely come looking for them. They exchanged anxious glances and whispered amongst themselves, tugging on each other's sleeves. He hadn't noticed them before, too intent on the rat to pay close enough attention.

The image of the blue-eyed girl flashed before him once more, her innocent face contorted into a chilling resemblance of Harrow's. He couldn't bear to make eye contact with the long, skinny boy who clenched his fist tightly in pain, standing beside the rat, or the children who blinked back tears. Mayhem quickly averted his gaze.

Bird. Alive.

Mayhem scoffed. The rat looked at him intently, ignoring the sharp glass shards that littered the space around them, and the child standing behind him in stunned shock.

Bird. Broken.

He shifted his weight onto one foot, testing his balance. Almost immediately, he stuck his wingtip out to catch himself as he wobbled, biting his tongue to keep from yelling out in pain.

The rat's eyes blinked several times.

"Harrow," Mayhem said at last, planting both feet onto the ground and hopping closer to the window. "She crushed my wings. I thought if I could get away from the house..."

The rat frowned, tail twitching irritably, front paws raised off the ground and resting in front of his chest. Like a squirrel, almost, without a nut. He didn't look as if Mayhem's discomfort bothered him at all. His paws tightened into balls, settling some deep, quiet thought.

In his peripherals, the boy stiffened, shoulders tensing. He took an unconscious step back, his gaze darting between the rat and Mayhem, mouth opened slightly as if to speak, but no words came out.

The bird's beady eyes flicked between the rat and the boy in confusion, until Mayhem remembered that birds didn't talk to humans. Not like that. The boy's fingers curled against his sides, uncertainty flickering across his face as he struggled to decide whether to run or stay.

Sharp words, simple and unspoken, echoed in Mayhem's mind, snapping his attention away from the scared child.

Bird, pet. Changed?

It hit like a slap, more than just a taunt, a judgment. Pet. The word gnawed at him, digging into his mind like Harrow's clawed hand.

Mayhem's wings flared, a pained stretch of muscle that sent a jolt of discomfort through him. The sharp hiss of his feathers, normally so fluid, faltered as they fumbled against the air. His talons scraped the floor, not with the usual strength, but with ragged desperation, as he tried to hold himself steady. Mayhem turned on the rat, the intensity of his gaze like a flickering flame, but the heat was tempered by the sharp, growing pain in his broken wing.

Pet.

Anger simmered beneath the surface, building in him like a storm, but the storm was off balance, disjointed. His chest tightened, breath coming in shallow, strained rasps.

"You—" he started, his voice a low, guttural growl, but it caught in his throat as his anger surged. The rat's eyes didn't flinch, even as the child at his side took a step back, hands up in instinctive defense, eyes wide and staring at him, before he realized how his old, croaking voice might have sounded to their delicate ears.

And still, the rat did not budge.

The silence that followed was thick. Mayhem's wings twitched with the weight of the pain now eating at him, the rage burning itself out in the quiet after his outburst.

He collapsed, ungraceful, his wings hanging limp at his sides, useless. The sudden release of tension left him feeling small, exposed. But the rat, that damn rat, didn't move a muscle.

Mayhem blinked slowly, his anger seeping into something else —something deeper, raw. Weak.

It was a strange thing, this exchange. The quietest of wars fought with only the smallest movements; no violence. Just a question, a look, and a truth that stung worse than any bite.

Mayhem closed his eyes and exhaled; his face shadowed with shame.

Girl. Died. You. Pet.

The rat's gaze raged with accusation, and Mayhem felt his feathers bristle.

Long, delicate strands of web began to stretch across the gaping opening in the window, overlapping and twisting together in intricate patterns. The silken threads glinted in the hazy glow of midnight, creating a mesmerizing display as they crisscrossed over each other until no trace of the gap remained visible.

As if on cue, one of the small girls stepped forward, her eyes locked on the jagged opening, pushing the boy with the bloody hand out of her way.

"Pia, stop! No!" The cry came, raw with panic, but Pia didn't even flinch. Her companion grabbed her arm, a silent plea hanging in the air, but the girl shook him off with a sharp twist. Determined, she broke away from the cluster of children, her movements deliberate and unyielding.

"This is it," she muttered under her breath, her voice trembling but resolute, as though the others had faded from existence.

With trembling hands, she gripped the edges of the shattered window. Crimson streaks blossomed as jagged glass bit into her skin, blood trailing down her pale fingers. She winced, but didn't falter. Shards scraped and cracked under her relentless effort, splintering away one by one. Each piece fell with a harsh clatter, the sound merging with her ragged, breathless grunts. Her resolve was terrifying, almost feral.

The girl's hands trembled with exertion, but she pushed through, driven by seemingly unyielding resolve. Blood dripped steadily onto the ground.

Almost a blood sacrifice.

And then she was free.

Mayhem, the rat, and the children stood frozen, their

eyes wide with disbelief. They watched in silence as Pia began to crawl through the small window, her determination evident in every calculated movement. Mayhem's heart raced as he wanted to scream at her, to stop her from what he sensed would come next—though he couldn't quite explain how he knew. The crow took a step backward, his beak agape, but no sound came out.

Webs came quicker now, snapping against Pia's skin and weaving faster. They were thin and gossamer, but their strength was undeniable as they tugged at her limbs and wrapped around her like a cocoon. Strands of silk tethered themselves to the glass edges, closing the gaps around her until she was completely ensnared. She was only halfway through the opening, deep gashes across her stomach from where the sharp fibers had cut into her flesh. Her blood dripped down the opalescent pane, creating macabre patterns, but there was no time left for her to escape.

Pia's breath came in shallow, uneven gasps, each one trembling with panic as the sticky, silken threads coiled tighter around her body. The strands glistened faintly in the dim light, their fibrous sheen betraying a strength far beyond anything natural. She clawed at them, her fingers slipping uselessly as the webbing constricted, digging into her skin with merciless precision. A strangled cry escaped her lips, cut off abruptly as the tension in the threads reached its peak. With a sickening, wet snap, the web sliced through her torso like a razor, dividing her in two. Blood sprayed in an arc, dark and glistening.

The silence that followed was deafening, broken only by the muted drip of her lifeblood soaking into the ground. It was only then, as her lifeless body collapsed into pieces, that the rest of them snapped out of their frozen stupor, moving at last—but far too late.

The air was heavy with the acrid, suffocating stench of death, a foul cocktail of decay that seemed to cling to every surface. It invaded the senses, turning each breath into a struggle, and left a bitter taste at the back of the throat. The smell was thick and pervasive, carrying with it the unmistakable tang of raw meat, mingled with damp earth and something sickly sweet that made the stomach churn. It was a scent that spoke of finality, of a life extinguished, and nature reclaiming what was once living.

It sent a wave of nausea and desire down Mayhem's throat again. His mouth was dry, his eyes frantic, finding no peace in the eyes of the children who cried in horror behind the windowpane, and nothing but disdain in the eyes of the rat, who tipped his snout up at the girl who now lay in two halves, scowling.

Door. Escape. None.

The window began its repair once more, weaving new silver threads across the fractured shards. Each strand thickened the barrier, dimming Mayhem's view of the rat perched on the other side. He pressed his snout close to the shrinking gap, his dark eyes narrowing.

Always. Hag. Always. Wins. Maze. Flea. Trapped.

The thoughts snapped like dry twigs, sharp and resigned. Flea bared his teeth, lips peeling back in silent fury.

Bird. Pet.

The word lingered, bitter. Then came the correction: **No. Game.**

Flea flicked his tail. If he turned his back now, it wasn't surrender—it was a judgment. A call to action, whether Mayhem responded or not.

The crow's gaze dropped briefly to the blood pooling below the sill, its metallic tang blending with the damp smell. Pia's remains, already forgotten. Flea's ears flattened as he turned, pushing off on his hind legs, retreating into the shadows.

But his thoughts lingered like an echo. A challenge, hurled across the webs that separated them.

It was a *game*. It was all-consuming for Harrow; a burning desire that coursed through her veins and fueled her every move. A relentless pursuit, a dangerous dance of predator and prey. The rush of adrenaline as she stalked her target, always one step ahead, knowing the thrill of the hunt would lead to an ever more satisfying victory. She lived for the game; it was her purpose and her passion. The chase was just as exhilarating as the ultimate reward that came from it—the satisfaction of outwitting and outmaneuvering the competition.

It was all about the game.

"Wait!" Mayhem called after him, though his voice was muffled by the thickening glass. Flea had no reason to hold, no reason to let the crow stop him from his escape into the house. But the rat paused, fur bristling along his neck.

The crow turned to face the open window atop the manor. "It's a game, rat. You need to think about the game; the one Harrow plays with us as pawns, but more importantly, the games we created for ourselves."

The one *only* meant for them. The crow, the rat, and the monster.

Mayhem watched as the hair smoothed along Flea's back, but the rat did not turn, as if he didn't have the same realization Mayhem did. With a flick of his tail, the rodent jumped from the windowsill and moved quickly within the darkness, the children still shocked into inaction, the rat dismissing Mayhem with his silence.

A silence that deafened with disappointment.

Chapter 15
The Rat

By this point, they were used to death.

But sudden death always arrests.

The children froze in shock, their grief so overwhelming and abrupt that it silenced their tears. Flea hurried through the winding maze, his every step urging his children to follow. Without a word, they fell in line behind him, slipping through the narrow corridors until they reached a small corner, just spacious enough for them to release the final, trembling waves of their sobs. Away from the event. Away from her corpse.

It was still too loud.

They weren't safe yet, Flea knew, casting several looks of disapproval towards the gaggle of tear-stained faces behind him. He would spend no time wasting on those he couldn't save any longer, the crow and the children included.

Flea shook his head, resisting the urge to bare his sharp teeth. They were too stupid to understand what Mayhem was trying to say to them—no, to *him*. He could see it in their blank stares. They didn't know what the crow meant, and what would come next.

Harrow loved the game; she loved it too much, and that would be her downfall. He was as much a part of it too, and that godforsaken crow, also.

Blue would have understood it immediately.

"This *isn't* a game!" The Lanky Boy with the bleeding hand, said in a voice that teetered just above a whisper, as if reading his thoughts. Flea turned to him as if he had spoken directly to the rat.

The boy's blood dripped steadily from his broken hand, crafting a trail that would lead Harrow right to them, if their voices that carried down the halls didn't first. Flea looked hard into the boy's eyes, wishing he could communicate with him.

Yes. Game.

There was no sign that showed the boy could understand him.

Flea tried again, willing the words so hard that he almost broke a sweat in his efforts.

Boy.

His eyes closed and his tail lashed around him. The children weren't listening.

They were pulling on each other's arms now, so hard that they nearly popped from the sockets. Groans of pain echoed across the dusted floors as they tried to drag one another in opposite directions, at odds as to where they would hide next.

"We have to try something—" Lanky Boy continued, "—the crow *talked*. It must be important. Didn't you see how he was talking to Flea?"

"Flea didn't say anything," Bear looked at the rat and then back to the boy. "He can't talk. Not like that."

"They were *talking*. I don't know how I know it; I just know it."

They would all be lost if they didn't move now. Not moving meant dying. Flea was close to disappearing into the walls again, leaving them to fend for themselves.

"Can't you just tell us what he meant?" Bear asked, his voice tinged with a mix of frustration and desperation. He crouched down slightly, extending his hand toward Flea as though coaxing a nervous animal. His fingers wavered in the cold air, trembling slightly with impatience.

The rat eyed him warily, his black, bead-like eyes glittering with defiance. Flea's fur bristled, and his whiskers twitched as he assessed the strawberry blonde boy's approach. When his hand got too close, the rat let out a low, guttural squeak and bared his yellowed teeth, the sharp points gleaming faintly in the dim light.

Bear flinched but pressed forward, determined. "Come on, Flea—"

Before he could finish, the rat scurried back several steps, his movements quick and precise, as though he'd anticipated the boy's lunge. His tail lashed against the ground like a whip, a clear warning.

Bear let out an irritated huff, straightening back up. Flea remained just out of reach, his small frame taut and ready to dart away at the first sign of trouble. He stared him down with an unsettling intelligence, as though silently mocking the boy's futile attempt to capture him.

Game. Bird. He screamed at Bear, but the boy wouldn't listen.

"You've got to help us!"

"He's a rat. He can't talk. And didn't you see how he left? The bird was basically screaming at him. Flea didn't listen, and I don't think we should, either."

The children exchanged uneasy glances, uncertainty flickering in their eyes like candle flames in a drafty room. But they nodded in agreement.

After a heavy silence, Bear let out a deep sigh and spoke in a low, steady voice laced with frustration. "Fine," he said, the edge in his tone undeniable. "Maybe the crow just thinks this is a game of hide and seek."

The words lingered in the air, dripping with mockery. Their expressions wavered between determination and doubt as they considered their next move. One by one, the children's gazes shifted to the boy with the delicate hands —a look all too familiar, one they'd once reserved for Blue —waiting for his command.

SKKRRRIIIIKKKKKKKTTTTTTT!

A loud, piercing sound ripped through the hallway, sharp and unrelenting. It echoed off the walls, ricocheting around them like it was alive, digging into their ears and thoughts. The walls began to undulate, their surfaces rippling as though they were preparing for something. The movement wasn't subtle; it was frantic, almost panicked. All around them the air grew heavy, tinged with an energy that made their skin crawl. Whatever was coming, the walls knew.

This wasn't Harrow—it couldn't be. The walls were moving too much for that, reacting as though they were scared, trying to recoil from what was approaching.

"What is *that*?" Lanky Boy whispered.

Flea's sharp eyes scanned beyond the group of children at the end of the hallway. At first, his vision was clouded by the dim light, but as he focused, a cold shiver ran down his wax encrusted back. Shadowy figures lurked within the darkness; their movements barely visible. The rat looked deeper into the hallway, trying to penetrate the gloom, and see the figures more clearly; to no avail.

It wasn't so much a figure, as a human-shaped mannequin, the first that appeared. It had no features on its face other than a sharpened row of teeth that sat in a wide-set mouth, stretching from ear to nonexistent ear. There were white eyes, no nose, no hair, just thick, uneven layers of wax coating its body, congealing in irregular drips down its neck and pooling at its joints like melted candle fat.

The wax clung to it in sickly, yellowed patches, obscuring parts of its form while leaving others grotesquely defined—long, spindly fingers gleamed under its dull sheen, stiff limbs encased in a shell that cracked and split with every unnatural movement.

The mannequin moved like a machine, its irregular flinches stopping only when the children looked in its direction. In the dim light, the wax appeared to glisten, as if perpetually in the process of hardening, trapping it in a half-finished state of decay. The only evidence of its movement was the creaking of the wooden floorboards and the echoes of sound as it planted its feet on the ground, leaving behind faint, tacky imprints where the wax had softened under its weight.

They were stuck in a dance—with each turn of their heads, another would move; and as the waxen mannequins shifted closer to them, their gruesome details cleared in the dim glow. Flea could better make out the crusted wax that layered atop their skin. He could see the opalescent, wet drool that dripped from their crusted lips; he could clearly define the details that made them Harrow's creations.

When the children turned their heads again, Flea stayed put, eyes zeroing in on a wax minion with no face.

Run!

He screamed at the children, knowing they couldn't hear him; that they wouldn't listen.

So, he ran.

Chapter 16
The Crow

THE SMELL OF DECAY WAS OVERBEARING.

Glass now sealed over the broken windowpane completely, leaving the splintered half of the dead girl to bake in the sunlight on the balcony beside him. Her guts spilled from her stomach, marinating in a pool of now boiling blood. Mayhem stood along the very edge of the platform, dancing on anxious feet. He couldn't stay clear of the girl's gore. As she lay, her blood spread, and it was close to covering the entire walkway. Flies caught wind of her stink, and the balcony Mayhem had risked his life trying to reach, became nothing more than a dirty place for him to die.

He hoped Flea had listened to him; the crow needed him to understand.

Mayhem kept his beak turned to the dead hills behind him, hoping no one would choose today to walk along the path that ran in front of the house—it would be a sore sight to see. Very rarely did a child die outside of the house on the hill. The crow couldn't actually remember the last time something like this had happened; he wondered if it was an indication that things were changing.

That pieces were falling into place.

Harrow was nowhere close to defeat, but her erratic behavior was cause for concern. If the woman made of wax died here, the crow felt so tethered to her that he feared he would go with her.

As if on cue, the platform below him started to tremble. It vibrated as if it was hungry; the world shaking around him so much that the crow could have very easily lost his balance and fallen off. He twisted his neck to look back at the child, but she was already half gone.

The balcony began to swallow her whole, pulling her body down like a predator consuming its prey. Weight from the wooden floorboards pressed into her flesh, leaving imprinted teeth marks on her skin. Like water pulled into a plughole, the draw of its throat drank her in. Had she been alive, she would have struggled against the pull, but it would have been no use—the balcony became an insatiable beast hungry for her. What remained of the dead girl was disappearing deep into the house like quicksand.

Mayhem staggered forward, his body moving without permission. He fought against it, but some wretched instinct overpowered him, dragging him closer to what was left of her. The scent of her blood, rich and seething in the heat, drowned his senses. He choked on it, trembled with the horror of it, but his body knew hunger like a wound that never closed. The crow's talons scraped through the slickness of her remains, his beak snapping forward as if on its own.

He tore a piece from her stomach, still warm, still wet.

Self-loathing curled through him as he chewed. Mayhem's throat spasmed, wanting to reject it, but he swallowed it down, bile and guilt burning at the back of his tongue. He could taste the child's last breath, an echo of her pain, and still, he took another bite. His body craved it, his nature demanded it.

By the time he ripped himself away, his beak was painted red.

Mayhem had done this. Not hunger, not Harrow, not the house—him. He was no better than the thing that had made him.

The crow's soul curdled inside of him, and he blinked, horror-stricken. He should have never stepped off that windowsill. Mayhem would rather spend over a hundred years watching the terrors of Harrow's victims before wanting to be alone like this again, becoming nothing more than a lost, hungry creature, as bad as the wax woman. In response, the empty silence of the estate mocked him, now settled from its meal, while his own stomach rumbled in satisfaction.

There was no reprieve for the children trapped here, and now there was none for him. As always, to him it seemed that the final fate of all who suffered the Hag's appetite was due to Mayhem, the crow who befriended the monster.

Who could love such a failure?

With darkness closing in around him, he perched at the edge of the platform, one foot poised to fall. He could still sense the invisible string that bound him to this place, a force beckoning him to come back to the windowsill, back towards the mayhem and madness.

So, the crow stepped off the balcony, with nothing between him and the ground but the fresh sounds of screaming children piercing the air.

Chapter 17
The Rat

When they ran, Harrow's wax demons gave chase.

Flea pressed himself close to the floorboards, and though he was well out of reach of their arms, it didn't seem like the wax figures wanted anything to do with him, anyway.

They chased only after the three children.

They were quicker than he could believe possible, and he realized that there was no world in which his children escaped their clutches. As more poured from the shadows, their mouths opened wide like Venus flytraps, their entire heads split in halves to devour whatever they could get their hands on.

The children sprinted through each devilishly decorated room and tried every old door, but everywhere they turned led to more creatures and more desperate flight. The house kept moving, shooting them back to where they started, right into the mannequin's reach.

Survive. Not. No. Run!

It didn't matter if they couldn't understand him. Flea screamed at them from inside his mind, as several more figures appeared, pulling themselves from the walls, itching to get free. To catch. To kill.

Flea ran as fast as his legs would carry him, his breath ragged as he weaved through the decaying hallway. The wallpaper peeled away in strips, attempting to snag and hinder, the air thick with dust, but he didn't dare slow down. The children's frantic footsteps pounded behind him, chased by the relentless clatter of their pursuers.

Then—a sharp gasp pierced the air. Greasy stumbled, his foot catching on a warped floorboard. A whimper escaped his lips. Greasy tumbled forward, arms flailing as he tried to regain his balance, but it was too late. With a heart-wrenching cry, he fell hard onto the ground, his eyes closing in fear as the wax demons closed in on him.

Flea skidded to a stop, heart hammering, as the figures loomed closer.

The other two children stopped in their tracks, torn between continuing their escape or going back to help their fallen companion. But the demons showed no hesitation; they lunged onto him with unnerving speed, their porcelain faces warped into grotesque expressions of hunger.

Flea watched in horror as the demons surrounded Greasy, their limbs creaking ominously, fresh wax pouring from open wounds. He knew that there was nothing he could do to save the child.

Their mouths opened, each one shoving a piece of the wailing boy into their jaws before chomping down, hard. Bones cracked, crushed by teeth, as his screams filled the air. Blood erupted from between clenched teeth.

CRUNCH. CRUNCH. CRUNCH.

Flea, feeling helpless, turned his head to keep from the worst of it, but his imagination couldn't escape the sounds that rang through the maze.

Lanky Boy and Bear clung to each other, unable to tear their eyes away from the grotesque scene unfolding before them. With one final, tearful glance at Flea, they slowly backed away, their footsteps echoing in the labyrinth, chased on their way by the bedlam of bones crunching, and Greasy's screams of agony. The boy was no match for the powerful, lifeless figures as they tore at him with sharp fingers and sharpened teeth, witnessed by their unfeeling, milky-white eyes.

And so, he died.

As the last breath of the boy left his body, the wax demons seemed to pause, their movements momentarily stilled. Flea shook, his throat constricted with grief. The room was eerily silent for a moment, only the panting of his breath and the flicker of the dim lights broke the oppressive silence.

Greasy's lifeless body slumped, discarded. As callously as they had taken it, they released him, to crumble against the cold, unforgiving wood, and Flea's heart wrenched in his chest. His soul screamed in protest, yearning to lash out and take back the horror that had occurred in this godforsaken place.

But he couldn't.

He was only a shadow, reduced to a mere observer in this sick, twisted game. The actual deaths of the children, he had always avoided, finally catching up with him.

He had now seen *two* of the children's gruesome deaths.

The wax on the mannequins began to drip and pool onto the floor, their faces distorting again into strange, empty expressions. It was as if life had been drained from them, satiated with their conquest, full from their last meal. They turned from what was left of the meat and muscle before them.

Flea stood with cemented feet, frozen in despair, as the mannequins turned their attention to their next prey. The children should have run like he begged them to. They could have been far from here if they had just listened to him.

Run!

They would be next, he knew. And then another, and another, until there was no one left, until the world was empty of light and hope. That was the plan, after all; to erase innocence from existence and leave only darkness behind.

Bear and Lanky Boy broke from their stupor, the same state that Flea desperately tried to shake free from, and used whatever they had left to run.

And again, as if the sudden movement turned them back on, Harrow's wax monsters moved and creaked to give chase, their arms reaching forward with stiff, unnatural grace.

Flea watched as the children moved too slowly, their strength waning with each passing second. The corridor stretched, unfurling in front of them, never quite letting them go where they wanted.

Flea was done moving. It didn't matter anymore.

This wasn't a game. It was carnage. The pretense of it all dropped—this was no single monster stalking its prey. It was the elimination of an infestation.

Their end was inevitable, just as the end of Greasy had been. Harrow's wax demons were relentless, their movements precise and unyielding. The children's lungs must have burned with every breath, the taste of terror and despair coating their tongues as they inhaled the caustic air.

Flea felt a tug in his chest.

It was like it had been there all this time, poking at him to notice, but he wouldn't. Instead of following the children and the demons that gained ground on them both, the rat wandered to the middle of the dusty hallway floor, closing his eyes.

It was faint, but it was there, a tiny, gilded string that tied him to something inexplicably *other*.

Harrow.

It had to be her; it had the same coating of dread, the stench of malice that he'd come to know so well. A rumble of recognition flowed through him, the humbled appreciation of the bond finally recognized, like he had gone on for too long without it. He was her eyes, here.

It filled the rat with overwhelming melancholy.

Come back to me, rat.

It was an order, not a suggestion. Despite the ruffled fur across his back from displeasure, the tug in his chest pulled harder, dragging him to the floor with a jolt. Flea blinked back tears. His head lifted from the wood, his tail fluttering against the floor in protest.

You can fight it all you want, Flea, but you will come to me in the end. Your children will not escape, the game is not built that way.

Try.

He begged. He had not resorted to begging throughout his entire life, but for them, for the children he'd already failed, he would beg.

Her voice sounded irritated, scratching at the inner walls of his ears, scorching his insides with her croaking voice.

If you must.

Irritation bled into disappointment, fading to a deep-rooted amusement as the rat finally opened his eyes and pushed himself upright. He ignored the tug in his chest, and it seemed to loosen the longer he denied it. The weight of Harrow was still there, not quite gone, but detached enough that he could focus again.

Harrow's callous laughs followed him as he came to, shaking his body and preparing to jump into another crook in the baseboards.

The rat's sharp eyes darted back and forth, scanning every inch of the abandoned maze. Each time he stepped on a creaky floorboard or shifted his weight, he felt Harrow's ever-present gaze, her scrutiny looming within him and weighing upon his wax crusted back.

The screams of the retreating children disappeared, soaking into the walls as if they never existed at all. The wax demons were gone, the last of his humans gone with them.

Harrow's voice grew louder, more insistent, and impatient.

I told you, rat.

Flea could feel her malevolent energy swirling around him like a cyclone. It was her design, after all. Ignoring the pain in his chest, Flea stretched out his claws.

This game was not meant for them. It was meant for you. You think I care about them?

The weight of his failure weighed heavily on his small shoulders. Despair returned with a vengeance, threatening to consume him.

I care about you, *Flea. About* Mayhem. *About* me. *These children? They are nothing.*

The darkness that had once terrified him now felt like a warm embrace in comparison to the pain he felt. Here in the maze, there was no escape. Harrow was the master. No matter how much he thought otherwise, she was the only player that could ever win.

The only real player in the game.

Tell me the truth, rat. How much longer can you do this? Put up this ruse? Like you're a martyr?

Flea squeaked in a quiet defiance, lifting his head before she shoved it to the ground with her invisible bond.

You are mine.

A thick veil of darkness descended upon him. It swallowed him whole, enveloping him in its suffocating embrace.

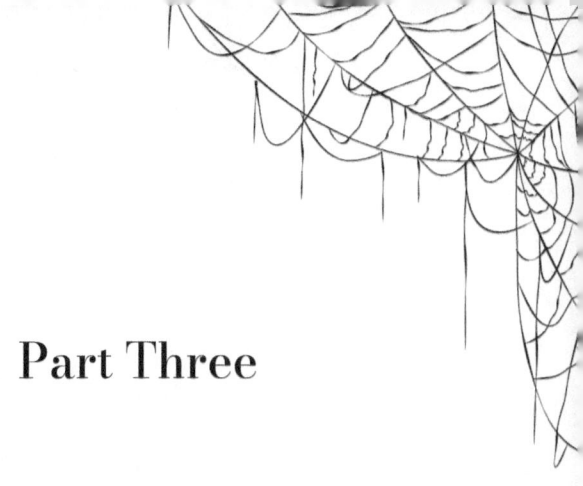

Part Three

"And this is why I sojourn here,'
        Alone and palely loitering,
    Though the sedge is withered from the lake,
        And no birds sing."

-La Belle Dame sans Merci: A Ballad, John Keats

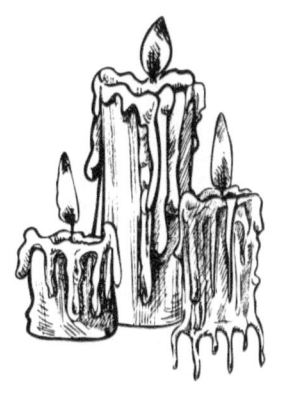

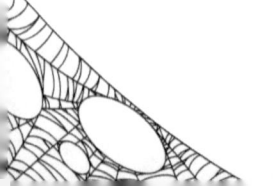

Chapter 18
The Crow

THIS FALL WASN'T LIKE THE LAST.

Much to his dismay, the crow wouldn't receive the satisfaction of a quick and painless death. Harrow made sure that it would be as drawn out as she could, just to taste his misery. To feast on his woe. To devour his melancholy.

He tumbled instead in slow-motion, the world around him moving so slowly that he could see every last detail of the house's rotted exterior and the dead hills around it. Every second seemed to stretch out into eternity as he fell, his body twisting and turning in the air; the wind rushed past him, tousling his feathers, his heart pounding in his chest—the only thing that seemed to be beating at a normal speed in this moment.

When Mayhem closed his eyes, he wished for it to end; yet, somehow, he knew she wouldn't allow it. As he hurtled towards his death—on his own accord—the crow cursed to himself. The draw to Harrow was as magnetic as ever, even as he dropped from the balcony. It lingered, pulling on him so hard that he thought he would snap back up and bounce from its elasticity. It wrapped around his soul, tugged until it suffocated him.

He was so close to the ground. To release.

Mayhem pictured Harrow's smile behind his eyelids, several rows of teeth sharpened and ready, flamed finger-tips curling to taunt him closer. There would be no light at the end of his tunnel, just complete darkness...

"It won't be that easy for you, bird." Her voice was as delicate as a whisper in his ears, but despite its softness, it was all-encompassing, echoing throughout his world.

And when he blinked, he was no longer falling.

For a moment, Mayhem panicked. Because what he saw when his onyx baubles scanned the room he now found himself in—the flickering flames of candles he'd only known surrounding Harrow's room—it sent him close to weeping. He didn't want to be back in the house; he didn't want to be stuck here, forced to witness every gory detail of her exploits.

Harrow was nowhere in sight, but the room pulsed with her presence, as if the very walls held onto the memory of her shape. The crow cautiously took a step forward, the floorboards creaking beneath his weight. Each sound echoed loudly in the stillness of the space, amplifying his unease.

But as Mayhem observed the room more carefully, he realized that there were things that were...askew. Small things, details that seemed off. The flickering candles cast dancing shadows on the walls, but those shadows moved in unnatural ways, twisting and contorting like they had a life of their own.

And then he heard their cries.

Beyond the doorway, closer than ever before, Mayhem

could make out the tattered sobs of the children in the halls. Normally, at this point, he would leave, hop onto the sill and fly off into the village. Around this time, he would abandon them to be found by the hag of wax, alone.

This time, he wouldn't leave them.

As the crow approached the door, it opened on its own. The air was thick with energy, pulsing and alive. A peculiar sense of both familiarity and the unknown washed over him as he stepped into the hall.

It was the first time he'd seen the other side of Harrow's door. The hallway stretched out before Mayhem, dimly lit by the same flickering candles that illuminated the room he had just left. Paintings adorned these walls, depicting scenes of beauty and horror in equal measure. Some portrayed serene landscapes bathed in warm sunlight, while others showed dark and twisted creatures lurking in shadowy corners. The colors were so vivid, they seemed to leap off the canvases, pulling Mayhem into their worlds; mesmerizing displays of human emotions captured in brushstrokes.

Prying his attention from the paintings, which seemed to move whenever he looked away, the crow tried to focus, though it was proving difficult. The walls moved, the decor rattled, everything was charged with dark, tendrilled magic. It pulled him in every direction, taunting him through closed doors and the shadowed holes in the walls.

Shadows reached out for him as he passed.

The cries of children grew louder as he was coaxed further into the hallway, their voices echoing off the walls to create an eerie cacophony that reverberated through Mayhem's body.

As he reached a particularly ornate door at the end of

the hallway, his clawed foot hovered uncertainly over the threshold, raised to the door.

With a deep breath to steady himself, Mayhem pushed it open and was met with a scene that made his heart drop to his talons. The room beyond was bathed in an eerie light that pulsed and flickered ominously. In the center of the room stood the source of the cries. Two small figures huddled together; faces stained from wet tears. Clung to one was the ripped scraps of what was left of a stuffed bear, the other's black hair had flattened to the top of their head, glued down by sweat. His long legs curled underneath him.

How many of the children had died?

Their eyes were wide with fear and their clothes were torn and dirty, the room bare and cold. And the rat was nowhere to be seen.

"We must go, now!" Mayhem squawked.

The fear and urgency in his tone spurred the children into movement. They quickly turned to face a door on their right and moved as one, a tightly knit unit working together to escape. He couldn't help but notice how hesitant each step was, how even the smallest sound forced them to look around wildly, as if they had been running from something that escaped from the walls. There was nothing around them now, but Mayhem was aware of how quickly Harrow's hallucinations could shift.

A shiver passed through his body. Of excitement.

She could drop whatever she wanted in front of them, like the toys she warned him of, and warp the world into her favorite torturous playthings. Mayhem followed closely behind.

"This was a game. You told us it was only a game," the boy with red hair tied into a knot, and the bear hanging loosely from his grip, cried. The other child hushed him, sending him into a fit of tears again, but the crow just cocked his head in sympathy.

It was cruel of him to keep it from them. They thought he meant that Harrow had been playing with *them*, that this was some grand trick meant for their wide, terrified eyes and trembling hands. But that was never the point. Harrow's game had never been for them. It had been for *him*, for *her*, for *Flea*. It had always been *theirs*. Her stolen children were only pieces, small moving parts within something much larger, something intricate and cruel, something that clicked into place with every choice, every movement.

The thought sent a shiver through him, not from fear but from recognition—an old, distant thing stirring at the edges of his mind, like a voice calling from the bottom of a well. A memory, dust-covered and waiting, suddenly shifting in the dark.

He swallowed hard, his beak clicking softly as he let the memory settle, let it root itself in the present. The boy was still crying, his breath hitching as the other boy whispered to him in a frantic, broken tone. Their fear made them small. It made them fragile. And Mayhem almost pitied them for it.

They were asking the wrong questions. Pleading for the wrong truths.

He shifted his weight, the old aches in his bones a quiet reminder of just how broken he still was. Harrow had always been like this—clever, cruel. Flea, too, though his cruelty was different, less deliberate. And him? He had been the observer. The hesitant one. The one who always wanted to believe there was still a choice, even when he knew better.

"It's only a game," Harrow told him often, her voice thick with something he hadn't recognized then—amusement, certainty, something like hunger. *"We play, and we see who wins."*

Back then, he hadn't asked what winning meant. He should have.

Because now, standing in the dim light with these trembling children, he understood—winning had never been about them. It had never been about who ran the fastest, who found the best hiding place, who followed the rules and who broke them.

The crow took a slow step forward, his head tilting as he looked at the children—not with sympathy, not really, but with something close to hunger. They wanted answers, something to cling to. But he could no more give them that than he could change what had already been set into motion.

The game had never been theirs.

And then came the creaking.

Soft at first, like old wood settling, like something shifting just beyond the veil of shadow. Then louder. Closer. Wax-stiffened joints of demons, sent from Harrow's horrific magic, groaned as they moved into view, their forms sluggish, unnatural. The scent of melted paraffin filled the air, thick and cloying.

One by one, they stepped into the dim light, emerging from the corners of the room, from the doorways and the blackened spaces between. There was no rhythm to their movement, only that eerie, jerking quality—like marionettes whose strings were being pulled by hands that didn't care for precision.

The children shrank back, their whispers turning to frantic gasps, then silence.

Wax demons surrounded them, their slick faces blank but for the occasional drip of congealed resin, that stretched and hardened like frozen tears. The candlelight flickered against their forms, highlighting the grotesque textures where the wax had pooled, where it had cracked, where it had melted away to reveal something almost human beneath—if human skin had ever been that pale, that still, that *wrong*.

Mayhem did not move. He did not flinch.

They wouldn't hurt him. They never would. The mannequins were as much a part of him as Harrow was. As Flea was. As the game itself was. And though they loomed now, their blank faces tilted just slightly toward him, he felt no threat in their presence.

The children, though? They had every reason to be afraid.

The first scream tore through the thick, stagnant air, so sharp and shrill that it made him wince—but only for a second. He let it wash over him, let it pierce the silence, then simply tuned it out. They never died quietly. There was always sound, always that raw, desperate edge of agony, and he had long since learned that it didn't bother him. If anything, it added to the anticipation. The wet, ripping sound of flesh parting followed soon after, nearly drowning out the choked sobs, the frantic gasps. That was always the way of it. Pain first, then fear, then the inevitable collapse into something primal. He exhaled slowly, already waiting for the scent to change, for the blood to bloom in the air like a thick, metallic perfume. The moment of transformation was coming. And he was ready.

The mannequins moved as one, lurching forward with unnatural speed, their wax-stiffened fingers closing around whatever they could reach—arms, throats, hair. Their bodies cracked with each motion, wax splintering like old candle husks, but they did not stop. They did not hesitate.

Mayhem didn't move. He simply watched.

The two children tried to crawl, but there was nowhere to go now. The demons sealed them in, their blank, faceless heads tilting as if listening, as if *learning*. One child was yanked backward so hard that Mayhem heard the sharp snap of a spine severing before his suddenly limp body hit the ground. The other boy with hair that mimicked his feathers clawed at waxen hands as they tightened around his throat, his desperate gasps lost beneath the rising wails of the other. The noises that emerged from his crushed throat were wet and coarse, the very act of swallowing air denied, his thrashing body desperate, as the sudden stench of ammonia flooded Mayhem's nares.

Blood splattered across the floor, a deep red that stood out against the demon's pale waxen forms. Their stiff fingers tore at flesh, peeling it back with a methodical kind of curiosity, as if unraveling the children piece by piece was just another part of the game.

Mayhem could no longer tell which noises belonged to whom. They had become a single, chaotic note in a symphony of breaking bones and gurgling pleas. The boy with the long legs still tried to crawl away, but a mannequin stomped down hard on his back, pressing him into his own pooling blood before tearing into his shoulder with its sharpened, wax-caked fingers.

Mayhem's eyes flicked over the scene, and something deep inside of him stirred again. Not horror. Not pity. Just hunger. And understanding. The mannequins were not cruel. They were not kind. They were only doing what they had always done, what they had been created for.

And Mayhem watched as long as he was able, until the

strength to close his eyes finally outweighed his desire to keep them open.

Mayhem wasn't even surprised that when he reopened his eyes, he was returned to Harrow's room again. His place on the sill was kept warm, the now present sun baking his back. Mayhem could not turn or twist his wings, but he no longer worried about pain. Harrow had broken him for a reason. He spread them wide and relished the feel of the grate of the bones, the splinters that pierced his skin. His black feathers were duller, his hope that had brightened the room now gone.

The room was the same as she had left it, lit by the escaping rays of sunlight illuminating the torn, wax encrusted carpet and the peeling walls. This was the house he remembered so well, the house that had molded him.

The crow saw her; the woman made of wax. She sat in the middle of the room. A table manifested before them both. He avoided her, skipping his eyes over her old, decrepit body as much as he was able, so long as he could focus on anything else; the floral print of the walls, the stench of death that assaulted his senses, the horrendous bout of wax that he could taste on his tongue.

"Mayhem, please, come down and eat with me."

She knew he was there. Of course she did. Harrow knew Mayhem's every move, every feather out of place. The woman made of wax owned him in every sense of the word. Yet she looked so pale. Frail. As if the violence of the centuries had finally taken its toll. He winced at the mention of his name, wishing he was able to ignore it, infuriated in a second that she should talk to him. Him, whom she had broken.

He could feel pangs of her annoyance echoing throughout the room. Yet they smelled different.

Almost as if they did not belong to her.

Between loud chewing sounds and the crunch of teeth tearing apart meat, she turned her face to look at him. There was a joy that lit the hollow pits of her sockets, a victory that radiated from her. He should have known she would come out on top. There was no chance for the children that were lured here to survive her; the demon Harrow had become in this world tore every little scrap of hope to shreds.

"I'll forgive your indiscretions if you join me," she pleaded still, before returning to her meal. Hunger rose in his throat, threatening to spill over.

His wings tucked into his sides and the crow had to take several deep breaths to calm his pain. He despised her in that moment, the way her very existence seemed to mock him.

The woman made of wax paused mid-bite, her gaze locking on something in front of her with hesitancy. She could sense the shift in the air, the rebellion brewing within the crow who had been her loyal servant for far too long.

"Mayhem, don't force my hand. Join me, or I will make you."

He couldn't resist the pull of her command, no matter how much revulsion it stirred within him. With a reluctant shift of his feet, Mayhem pushed off the sill and opened his wings to glide in agony towards the wooden table at which

Harrow sat. He landed on it like dead wet meat, his ribs snapping and shifting, his lungs seizing in dread. Yet still he rose, and slowly hopped closer to the table, his black eyes fixed on the grotesque feast spread out before Harrow. The remnants of innocence lay scattered on delicate china plates, mingling with the stench of decay that permeated the air. Next to the plates, a teddy bear sat as if in observation, mute.

As he perched on the edge of the table, she reached out a hand with fingers like melted candles, their tips glowing softly in the dim light of the room. He flinched instinctively, wary of her touch, but she only used her flamed tips to offer him a morsel of the grisly meal before her.

"Come now, my faithful companion," she cooed, her voice like honey and venom intertwined. "Partake in this exquisite feast with me. It is not every day I have such delightful company."

Mayhem's beady eyes flickered between the woman and the remains on the table, his mind swirling with conflicting emotions. The thought of consuming the flesh of the boy was a torment, no matter how much his mouth watered. Yet he would no longer deny his nature.

The crow pecked at the offered morsel, letting the wave of revulsion wash off him as he tasted the sweet metallic tang. Saliva pooled in his beak.

"A familiar never betrays their master. Even if he wanted to. You think I didn't know what you were up to? That was foolish of you, bird. Reckless, stepping off that ledge. And now, you will eat his remains. You will carry this boy inside of you as a reminder of what happened when you failed me."

Harrow's words hung in the air, her voice a sibilant hiss that echoed in Mayhem's mind long after she had stopped speaking. The walls of the house, never once familiar or homey, closed in on him, as he was reminded of his place within the house's twisted realm.

The sun that had shone through the windows disappeared, leaving nothing behind but cool winds of comfort. Harrow was the keeper of everything that happened here, and that reach was all-encompassing.

"You really think you had a choice?" Her laugh surprised him, like she had been reading his thoughts. "You thought you had free will? Never. There was no part of this home—*our home*—that would let you go. You are tethered here, Mayhem. You are tethered to *me*."

"A cruelty you will never outdo," he hissed in return.

Harrow pushed the last of the meat on her plate with her fingertips, leaving dried wax to soil it.

"I never thought my familiar, *my blood*, would be this petulant."

The bond between them felt strained and frayed, like a rope ready to snap at any moment, and the weight of the boy's remains within him served as a reminder of the consequences of his actions. Mayhem held Harrow's gaze, defiance burning in his dark eyes. Despite the fear and despair swirling within him, there was a spark of rebellion that refused to be extinguished. He knew he had ventured too far, challenging the very core of their bond. But as much as he tried to push back against Harrow's control, he was bound to her by ancient magic and an unbreakable oath.

"There is not much you can do, Mayhem. You cannot kill me. You cannot thwart me." Harrow's lips curled into a cruel smile, her amusement at his defiance evident in the sharp glint of her eye sockets.

"But you *can* tell me what happens now," she continued. The wax woman's eye sockets bore into the crow's, a chill running down his spine.

Mayhem squawked in protest, his wings beating nervously against the edge of the table, heat radiating from his broken limbs. He knew the cost of his actions could be devastating, but he couldn't bring himself to let go of the boy, the blue-eyed girl, or the children that came before them.

Harrow leaned back in her chair, the seat creaking ominously. She reached for a nearby candle that was not her fingers, its flame a bright orange glow. With a slow, deliberate motion, she set the candle down on the table, the heat immediately causing the candle wax to melt and drip, merging with the bones that littered the tabletop. Harrow's eye sockets never left Mayhem, a devious smile playing on her lips.

"And now," she whispered, her voice laced with satisfaction, "you will carry the guilt of your actions with you. You will feel it in your blackened heart and in the feathers that hold your soul together. And you will never, ever, fight your own nature."

The birdcage behind her seemed to shimmer in the corner. The intricate golden bars and delicate engravings—a stark contrast to the plain wooden table she sat at—caught his attention and pulled it away from Harrow's malicious intent. As Mayhem studied the ornate, gilded cage, a fresh sense of unease washed over him.

There was something off about the way the golden bars seemed to glow too brightly, almost as if they were pulsating with unnatural energy. Glancing back at the woman seated at the table, he noticed her unnerving smile and the knowing glint in her eye sockets. Without a word, she reached out and beckoned the cage closer.

A terrible, screeching sound of metal sliding against the floor echoed as she forced it to succumb to her will. Harrow waved her hand and opened the cage door, releasing a flurry of shimmering golden dust that swirled around the room in a hypnotic dance.

"Come, Mayhem. Do not waste any more time with your fruitless endeavors."

The crow peered inside with a heavy heart. A profound sadness washed over him, an ache that seemed to settle into his very bones, knowing it would linger for years to come. He understood that this was the end, the inevitable fate that had been laid out before him. The bars of the cage loomed around him, casting shadows that seemed to stretch across the room.

"I do not mean to say that this is the end." Her voice was lower now, gentler. It was as if she genuinely cared for him, as if his hurt softened her. "You are like me, malleable wax that can withstand the test of time. While I live, so will you. You can be new again."

Mayhem cocked his head to the side, his sharp beak slightly agape to taste the stale air.

With a hesitant flutter of wings, Mayhem ventured into the cage. Within moments, he felt the warm embrace of Harrow's magic as it seeped into his feathers, filling him with a newfound strength. No longer was he weighed down by guilt. As Mayhem stood in the embrace of the golden cage, he could hear the wax woman's words echoing in his mind. "While I live, so will you."

And so, he did.

Within the gilded bars of the cage, fire sparked from the tips of his wick-ed wings, fresh wax pooling below his feet, like he was transforming into a crow shaped, wax shelled version of *her*.

Harrow watched with a satisfied smirk, her waxen features betraying a sense of pride at the creation she had wrought.

"My loyal companion," she whispered, her voice a soft caress that belied the darkness within. "Let us wait for our third to arrive."

Chapter 19
The Rat

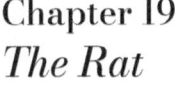

Flea wandered the halls of Harrow's decrepit maze, his small claws clicking softly against the aged wooden floor. The walls breathed in, shifting ever so slightly in the dim candlelight.

He had been running for so long. Hiding. Surviving.

This wasn't just a game of evasion—it was something deeper. A cycle, a lesson written in the bones of the house itself. He trailed his paw along the peeling wallpaper, the sensation of decay under his touch sending a shudder down his spine.

The corridors twisted upon themselves, a maze of forgotten rooms and hallways that led to nowhere. A broken mirror caught his reflection in its jagged teeth, the glass warping his image, making his eyes seem too large, his form too small. The air held a scent—mildew, old wood, and something faintly metallic. Flea pressed forward, his breath shallow, ears twitching at every creak and groan of the house.

Somewhere beyond the next doorway, he knew Harrow was waiting. Watching. The game was nearing its end, but

Flea no longer feared it. Understanding had begun to settle in his bones, like a long-forgotten memory resurfacing. The rules could be changed. The roles could be swapped.

The thought struck him like lightning. He paused, his tiny chest rising and falling in quick bursts. It was never about just running. It was about balance. The hunter could become the hunted. The cycle could be broken. If only he dared to act.

Taking a deep breath, he stepped into the next room, its walls draped in tattered fabric, shadows dancing like ghosts. And there, in the center, one of Harrow's wax demons loomed. A towering, monstrous figure, eyes gleaming like distant stars. But Flea did not cower.

Harrow?

He spoke to the figure as if it would speak back to him, like it would listen.

The wax demon lifted one stiff, clawed arm and pointed to the far wall. Flea's breath hitched as the wallpaper peeled back, the wood groaning as a door appeared where none had stood before. It was old, warped, with a rusted brass handle that seemed to pulse faintly, as though alive. From beyond it came the unmistakable sounds of cracking bones, of wet squelching and shrill squawks, sounds of something being torn apart, devoured.

His fur bristled. He knew what lay beyond. Harrow and the crow. Waiting.

Flea stepped forward cautiously, his heart hammering against his ribs. The door seemed to call to him, something about it tugging at his insides. He pressed his nose to the aged wood, inhaling the scent of damp sweetness. As if responding to his presence, the door groaned open, its hinges shrieking like something long dead waking up. The room beyond was dimly lit, shadows pooling in the corners.

At the center of a wooden table sat Harrow, watching him with her unreadable eye sockets. And nearby, in a rusted gilded cage, was something that could have been the black bird he had found earlier—its feathers slick with something wet, its form trembling.

But Flea felt at home.

Harrow's presence clung. It dripped along the walls and flowed across the wooden floors like slow, melting wax. Flea could *feel* her. The woman made of wax infested the maze; the room shuddered under the heaviness of *her*.

Wispy strands of mist enveloped them, drifting and settling through the room like fingers. As if they walked through a dream, their surroundings remained obscured and hazy, the air damp and cool against their skin. She looked just as gruesome as he remembered, even more so with each reacquaintance. Dried milky droplets of wax covered her entire face, yellowed from years of aging. Harrow's cheekbones were high and well pronounced, with points so sharp they could cut through skin, her hallowed sockets so deep, it was like looking into a void.

Game.

Flea stared past her grotesque features, focusing on the holes in her head where her eyes should have been. He watched lone spider webs swinging in their depths as her head cocked to the side, but he spoke to her with conviction. He was in no state to draw this out any longer than she had already.

"I don't play games with rats." She growled. The bird in the cage cawed, but the rat ignored him.

Understand. Harrow.

She was unused to hearing her name aloud. The house rattled around them, pulsating in sync with her heart, but Flea could see the spark of interest settling into her posture.

Harrow's jaw shortened; her teeth sank slowly back into her gums. She pushed back in her chair and stood.

"I see."

Bird. Game. Harrow. Game. Flea. Game. All. Game.

He faced Harrow boldly, his gaze locked onto hers with steely determination. A silent understanding passed between them. There was no turning back now as they stood on the edge of a precipice, ready to leap into the unknown. The intensity of their shared moment hung in the air, crackling with energy like a storm brewing on the horizon.

Her slow smile was worse than the rat's nightmares. Harrow raised her hand dramatically, magic crackling at her beck and call. She rubbed her fingers together, creating a static that electrified the room as she snapped.

"Tell me, Fleabag," her voice was louder now, more menacing, "Don't be shy now. What did it take for you to figure it out?"

Gathering every ounce of strength he possessed, the rat met Harrow's hollow gaze with a steely resolve. Harrow's laugh flowed through him, malevolent cackles rooting themselves in his body until they crashed against his ribcage, cracking the already frail, weary bones.

Harrow tilted her head, her grin widening, as if she could peel back the rat's skin with just a look. "Oh, come now," she crooned, her voice dripping with mock affection. "Don't tell me you had help. That would be such a disappointment."

Indiscernibly, Flea looked at Mayhem briefly, then back to Harrow.

She took a step closer, her shadow swallowing him whole. "Or did you simply get tired of being afraid?"

The rat's breath came in sharp, ragged bursts. His body

screamed for retreat, but something deeper—something desperate—pushed him forward, to end it before she could see what was happening.

He leapt, paws outstretched, and pressed against Harrow's waiting hand.

I win.

The air rippled, reality fracturing as the illusion peeled away. The walls of the house dissolved, revealing something beyond—a landscape teeming with fragile life.

Life, slow and cautious, but real.

He was sure he was dreaming. The light backdrop before him was a stark difference from the darkened brown and dusted glow that he'd been forced to endure for years. Sunshine stretched across the sky with white strings of clouds sprinting across the expanse, fleeing its bright, incessant rays. What remained was a delicate but piercing color the same as Blue's eyes, and it was too painful to keep his attention for more than a moment. Guilt dropped into the rat's heavy belly, a monster chewing at his insides. It would be a constant reminder of the pain he'd caused, and the consequences of his selfishness.

Flea shielded his eyes from the blinding light. As his vision continued to adjust, he realized he was standing in a vast field of dead wildflowers, swaying gently in the warm breeze, each stem cracking and falling to the ground. The scent of dying buds filled the air, and the sound of the crow nearby heightened his senses. He turned around slowly.

It could have been Harrow's trap, but if it was, she had crafted it to be too raw and unseasonably real. He felt everything around him, and the warmth that seeped into his bones was not a figment of his imagination.

Flea was too entranced, Harrow's glamour peeling back

to reveal a world that was growing and becoming new again. A world Harrow hid from them all.

And then—he *fell.*

Not in body, but in mind, slipping into something vast and terrible. He was no longer himself. He was *her.*

The world stretched out before him, vibrant and full, but *wrong.* Too loud, too alive, too unbroken. He—*she*—stood at the center of it, staring at the pulsating heart of a thing that had not yet learned to suffer. And that would not do.

Hunger curled inside him. Not the mindless, gnawing kind that Mayhem carried, but something colder. Something deeper. The need to break. To unravel. To take this world apart until only bones remained.

The first thing to go was the light. He tore the sun from the sky with a thought, leaving it smoldering on the horizon, a dying ember. Darkness came next, stretching long and thick across the land, swallowing the faces of those who screamed in confusion. Their cries were music—*Harrow's* music.

Then the rivers dried, leaving only cracked earth where water had once danced. The forests curled in on themselves; the trees shriveling to brittle husks. He could feel life leaving the world, drawn into his waiting hands. *Her* hands.

It was *beautiful.*

But beauty never lasted.

As the last echoes of the world faded, Harrow had waited. Not out of regret. Not out of sadness. But because the game could not start if nothing remained to play it. And so, she sat among the ruins, watching, listening, letting the silence stretch until it became unbearable.

Only then did she allow the world to heal.

Not fully. Never fully. Just enough for life to claw its way back. For the land to remember what it had lost and still dare to hope. That was the cruelest part of all—hope.

That was when she made the game.

A labyrinth of misery and survival woven from the remains of what had once thrived. She had crafted it carefully, piece by piece, ensuring it would never grow dull. There would always be struggle. Always pain. Always something to watch. *She had spent centuries perfecting it.* Because what was the point of power if there was nothing left to toy with?

Flea gasped, the memory tearing itself from his body like claws raking down his back. He staggered, heart pounding, his mind reeling from what he had seen—what he had *been.*

Harrow's monstrous form shuddered, then shrank. Her limbs curled inward, her massive frame twisting, reshaping, until all that remained was a rat. Small. Vulnerable. From all that she had destroyed, she could only regret. Regret her fun was over. Shame for what she had destroyed —her darting eyes avoiding any hint of accountability. She would run. She would hide. She would survive.

From the darkness, Mayhem emerged, his grotesque form shifting with a hunger deeper than mere appetite. He had been broken, betrayed, his monstrous existence a testament to survival at any cost. His impartiality and guilt had brought him nothing. All that was left was rage, and the knowledge he, she, was unloved.

The gilded cage shattered as she grew. She would consume because she had to, because it was the only way she knew. And yet, in the depths of her hunger, there was something else—longing. Desperation. A need for something more than just destruction.

She settled into her new, yet eerily familiar form,

inhaling as if savoring the moment. Her hands rose to her face, trembling slightly—not with hesitation, but with something deeper, something primal. Through Harrow's features, Mayhem's eyes gleamed, alight with recognition and madness.

Slowly, deliberately, she stretched her fingers before her, flexing them one by one. As they curled, fire bloomed at the tips, small at first, then flaring into hungry tongues of orange and blue. The flames crackled and danced, casting erratic shadows across her stolen face. Heat shimmered in the air between them.

She grinned, her lips parting to reveal teeth too sharp, too eager. Her gaze lifted to Flea, unreadable yet brimming with something final.

"Nothing left to see," she whispered, voice rich with something between amusement and resolve.

Then, without hesitation, she plunged her burning fingertips into her own eyes.

A sickening sizzle filled the air as fire met fluid, and steam erupted from the sockets in thick, curling plumes. The gelatinous mass of her eyes boiled and melted, running in viscous, smoking trails down her cheeks. Her cry rang out; not of pain, but of something deeper, something raw and triumphant. It was a sound both terrible and exultant, reverberating through the space as the flames consumed what was left.

Flea watched, but the horror he expected to feel never came. No revulsion twisted his gut, no instinct urged him to recoil. Instead, he felt... nothing. Or perhaps something worse than nothing. A quiet understanding, a recognition that settled deep in his marrow.

And then the change began.

A shuddering shift that began in his bones and unfurled

outward. His fur prickled, darkening, hardening, until it became sleek black feathers. His limbs stretched, hollowing, reshaping, his claws curling into talons that scraped against the air. His spine arched, lengthening, his body light as the wind itself.

A great weight lifted from him as the last remnants of his rat form melted away and his bones hollowed. The walls that once caged him—the suffocating corridors of shadow and despair—receded into nothingness. No longer bound to the ground, he lifted into the sky, wings cutting through the air with newfound grace.

Yet the guilt...

Like a chain on his heart, its cord snapped around him like chicken wire. He was running again.

Had he learnt nothing?

As real as a leash, he knew he could not leave the hag to carry out her despicable nature without witness. Screaming into the wind of his so-near freedom, the crow launched himself through the window.

Just to taste the freedom. For a second.

Below, the world shifted, but he did not. He was above it now, apart from it. Watching. Remembering. He cawed, wings trembling. Flea had spent so long learning to survive; now he had to learn something else, to understand the cycle that never truly ended.

Harrow, now reduced to a small, trembling rat, darted away with frantic haste, her tiny form weaving between the scattered shadows. She had committed atrocities. Her own nature had overwhelmed her. And the poor children...

The sleek fur of her new shape caught the dim light, but there was no disguising the desperation in her movements, no hiding the power she once held now lost to something smaller, weaker. She was fleeing, but for what?

That would be her name. Flea... from now on, until she could remember...

from what...

Even as the rat skittered into the dark, the faint echo of her fear lingered, cold and hollow.

What had once been Mayhem, the grotesque and twisted thing that was once more the hag, let loose a guttural growl from deep within her chest, the sound like gravel scraping against bone. Her eye sockets glinted with a feral hunger, wide and unblinking, as her monstrous limbs moved with unsettling precision. She took a step forward, each movement a heavy promise of destruction. Her body, an ugly patchwork of beast and rage, rippled with power as she stalked toward the shadows where Flea had disappeared, a predator preparing to hunt.

High above, Mayhem watched the unfolding scene, his sharp eyes tracking every motion, every shift. His wings spread wide, trembling with the knowledge of what had come before, of what was about to unfold. The world beneath him pulsed with purpose, but he was untethered. The lesson was beginning again.

He would learn. And he would remember.

When the time came—when the cycle's course had played out and the thread was woven through his being once more—he would take his turn. He would carry the weight of what was lost, and what must always be regained.

The game was not over.

It was only beginning again.

Playlist

- **Vermillion** - Slipknot
- **Change (In the House of Flies)** - Deftones
- **So Cold - Remix** - Breaking Benjamin
- **Sober** - TOOL
- **Prelude 12/21** - AFI
- **Wasteland** - 10 Years
- **Spiders** - System of a Down
- **Lonely Day** - System of a Down
- **Falling Away from Me** - Korn
- **Rats** - Ghost
- **The Red** - Chevelle
- **Vermillion, Pt. 2** - Slipknot

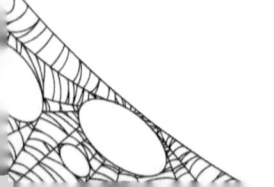

Acknowledgments

I started writing this book because it was the first time in years that I felt like the story *needed* to be written. I don't know how people will respond to my broken critters, and I don't know how they will understand this bleak tale of a woman tearing apart children because she craved love. Harrow, Flea, and Mayhem were born out of loneliness, regret and *hunger*. And it scares the shit out of me that people are going to read this.

At least I have a community around me that supported its creation.

Thank you to my cover designer Pia @crimsonsdesigns, my editor Austrian Spencer @austrianspencer, and my proofreader Candace Nola @cnola.author. As always, bringing a book to life requires partnership and collaboration with so many other artists that are geniuses in their craft.

To my partner, Gabriel. Though this year brought us so many new challenges to navigate, what we found was a deep love for horror together. Thank you for following me to conventions, and for respecting and cherishing the time and memories we were able to create because of this genre.

To Katelyn, who probably threw up a few times reading this, and for being the biggest support system I could ever ask for.

To Tiff, who is just along for the wild ride, even if there's no real love story in it. I love you endlessly.

To the following authors: Royal Poff, Cat Delani, Clay McLeod Chapman, Sam Rebelein, Todd Keisling, Ben Farthing, William F. Gray, A.G. Mock, Joseph Pesavento, Dorian Sinnott, Patrick Tumblety, Adam Cesare, and Ronald Malfi. For being friends, mentors, and the most incredibly talented people I know.

To Mike DeCesaris. Thank you for being someone that makes me feel like writing is the right call, always.

To Delta. Every single time.

To Troop, who welcomed me with open arms when I needed it most.

To my Patreon members, who have supported me in more ways than I ever expected: Z, Sarah, Crys, Rob, Skye, K.C., Cat, Wavel, Pia

To Killer Bestsellers and Twins and Talent, for being the best teams for this book. It was in excellent hands because of you.

And as always, thank *you*, reader. I hope you find love within these pages beyond the horror.

About the Author

Cassandra Celia (she/they) is a Maryland bookseller, turned author. They write gothic, horror, and dark fiction, such as THE ELRIC UNDOING, and her latest release, HOUSE OF HARROW. Cassandra obsesses over stories with love, death, ambiguous endings, and everything in between. In their books, she takes inspiration from haunting art and media, and she absolutely loves writing about angry, scorned women.

Stay up to date by visiting their website, www.cassandracelia.carrd.co.

facebook.com/authorcassandracelia

instagram.com/authorcassandracelia

tiktok.com/@authorcassandracelia